LOON ISLAND

Published by Lobster Press™
1620 Sherbrooke Street West, Suites C & D
Montréal, Québec H3H 1C9
Tel. (514) 904-1100 • Fax (514) 904-1101 • www.lobsterpress.com

Publisher: Alison Fripp
Editor: Mahak Jain
Editorial Assistants: Stephanie Campbell & Simon Lewsen
Graphic Design & Production: Tammy Desnoyers
Production Assistant: Vo Ngoc Yen Vy

 Canadian   Patrimoine
Heritage   canadien

We acknowledge the financial support of the Government of Canada
through the Canada Book Fund for our publishing activities.

Library and Archives Canada Cataloguing in Publication

Gamache, Donna Firby, 1944-
    Loon Island / Donna Firby Gamache.

ISBN 978-1-77080-070-0

    I. Title.

PS8563.A5716L66 2011   jC813'.54   C2010-906439-9

Brink's Truck is a trademark of Brink's Inc.; **Coleman** lantern is a trademark of
Coleman Company, Inc.; **Ontario Provincial Police** is a trademark of OPP Ltd.

Printed and bound in Canada.

*With thanks to my husband, Luc Gamache,
for his support while I was writing this book.*

– Donna Firby Gamache

LOON ISLAND

written by
Donna Firby Gamache

Lobster Press ™

CHAPTER 1

ALEX MARCHED TO the front of the launch, leaving his mother alone with his twin sisters. The horn blared a warning and the boat pulled away from the Kenora dock.

He didn't bother looking back at the people waving on the shore. What would be the point? No one was there to wish him good-bye. And he was fine with that. He didn't want anyone to know that Alex O'Grady was being forced to go on vacation this close to home – on an island in the Lake of the Woods.

Instead, Alex fixed his eyes on a motorboat carrying three fishermen. As the launch turned, he caught sight of the dock from the corner of his eye. Yup – people looked pretty dumb waving their hands like that.

When Alex's mother told him that she'd booked a week at Family Camp, he had fought against the idea. "Can't we at least go somewhere farther away? Anywhere but this lake? Loon Island is hardly more than half an hour by boat from Kenora."

Going only half an hour away meant that he was sure to meet people who knew his family. And if they didn't know his family, they would recognize his family's last name.

"I've already booked a week off work from the restaurant," his mother replied with a sigh. "And Family Camp is the only thing we can afford. Hotels cost too much."

"How about going camping? Camping's not so expensive."

"We don't have the equipment. You know that. And we'd have to drive to a campground somewhere. The car's likely to break down any minute."

After that, Alex kept his feelings to himself. It was going to be a long week. Especially since he knew his mother had other plans for this vacation. She'd been talking to the school counselor after Alex barely passed into ninth grade. Ever since then, she kept going on about how Alex needed to "work through some things."

"It's been nearly three years," she'd said to him just two nights ago. "You've got to stop pushing everyone away. The only person you're punishing is yourself." A week with her lecturing him, trying to dissect him, didn't sound like much fun.

But it hadn't *all* been his fault. He *had* pushed people away, but some of them had stopped talking to him on their own. Daryl, the last of his friends, was one of those people. Or maybe it was

Daryl's parents who'd broken up their friendship. Alex didn't know why Daryl had ditched him, but he no longer cared.

He had learned over the past three years that he was better off without any friends. He kept a low profile. He didn't get into any fights and he didn't talk to anybody who didn't talk to him. Most days he had to babysit after school anyway, until his mom got home from working at the steakhouse.

Now, looking over the boat's passengers, he counted about fifty people on board, young families mostly, headed for Family Camp. Only one person looked to be around Alex's age, a dark-haired boy standing at the back of the launch. He was clutching a small digital camera to his chest. Every now and then he snapped a photograph.

Alex eyed him from afar, but he had already decided he wouldn't go over to say hi. He had become used to people not wanting to talk to him, at least those people who knew about his father. These days, he didn't even try to make new friends.

As soon as the boat pulled away from the docks, though, the boy came to stand beside Alex. He wore a plaid, button-up shirt instead of a T-shirt. His skin looked as if it hadn't seen much sun.

"Are you going to Family Camp too?" he asked.

"Uh, yeah," Alex said. "That's the only place

this boat's going today."

"I didn't know that. I'm not from around here. My name's Jerry – Jerry Wylie. From Winnipeg."

"I'm Alex." He left his last name off on purpose. Winnipeg was over a hundred miles away, but the boy might still recognize his family's name from the news.

"Where are you from?"

"Just back there in Kenora." Alex hesitated. He didn't want to reveal too much. The more you said, the more questions people asked. "That's my mom and sisters at the back." He indicated a tall, reddish-haired woman sitting with two blond girls in sundresses.

Jerry took a picture of Alex's family and then turned back to Alex. "I'm thirteen," he said. "Fourteen in a few weeks. How old are you?"

"Fourteen."

Jerry nodded. "I figured we'd be the same age. So why's your family taking a holiday so close to home?"

Kind of a nosy guy, Alex thought. "Because it's cheap and meals are included."

Jerry waited for Alex to say more. When he didn't, Jerry pointed to a couple standing near the side of the boat. "Those are my parents," he said. The man was tall and slim, with blond hair. The woman had darker hair and looked more like her son. She clung nervously to the edge of the boat. "My mom is scared of boats," he explained. "We practically had to drag her onto this one."

"Have you been here before?"

Jerry shook his head. "We just moved to Winnipeg last Christmas. We used to live in southern Saskatchewan – not many lakes there." He paused. "Do you like living around here?"

"There's good swimming. Good boating. Good fishing. If you like that sort of stuff ..."

Jerry didn't seem to notice that Alex hadn't answered his question. "Do you fish? My dad wants to try it while we're here."

"Not lately. My mom doesn't like it." Alex looked away.

"What about your dad?"

Alex fixed his eyes on a seagull overhead. "My dad's dead."

"Oh." For some minutes there was an uncomfortable silence as the boat slid past several dark green islands. Then Alex broke the tension by pointing ahead.

"Look – we're at the Devil's Gap."

"The Devil's what?"

"The Devil's Gap. It's the channel between those two islands. The water's supposed to be deep."

"Is it dangerous?" asked Jerry. He sounded nervous now. Alex noticed that Jerry was clinging to the railing as tightly as his mother.

"Nah, not really. I think they just want to make it sound that way. And look over there."

The launch slowed and turned toward a large solitary rock perched on an island. It was shaped somewhat like a broad head. The rocky face glared at the boys in the harsh afternoon light. It was decorated with ghostly white eyes, a gaping mouth, and slashes of war paint. Alex had seen pictures of the rock in posters around Kenora – he'd even been past it once when he was younger – but seeing it again still made him shiver.

"It's the Devil's Rock," he explained. "There are different legends about it. Some people say that a band of Cree had a battle near here and several were killed in an ambush as they canoed past. Others just say three guys painted it for a joke way back in the olden days."

"Really? That's cool." Jerry relaxed his hold on the railing. "Which story is true, though?"

"Who knows? Probably the second one. But now it's just kept for the tourists. Boatloads come out from Kenora to see it."

"It looks scary enough," Jerry admitted as the launch eased its way past the eerie face staring down at them. He lifted his camera and snapped a picture. Then he pulled a small notebook and pen from his back pocket and started writing in it. "I keep track of anything interesting – or suspicious – that I see," he explained. "I'm training to be an investigative journalist."

Weird guy, Alex thought.

Jerry tucked the notebook and pen back into his pocket. The two boys moved closer to the bow to catch the wind while the boat rumbled back up to speed.

"I can see why they call it the Lake of the Woods," Jerry said. He pointed to several islands bunched together. Each one was a miniature forest floating on a bed of blue. "How many islands are there, anyway? I stopped counting after the first fifteen."

"Thousands," Alex said. "Depends on what you call an island, though. Some are quite big, but others are just rocks with enough soil for about one tree. The tourist guide says there are more than fourteen thousand islands altogether."

"Wow. How big is the lake?"

Alex tensed. Questions about the lake and things that had happened on it were dangerous territory. "It's nearly seventy miles long and almost as wide," he said. "Part of it's in Ontario and part of it's in Minnesota. It just doesn't seem that big because of all the islands."

"What about Loon Island? Have you been there before?"

Alex clutched the side of the boat. *Just another innocent question*, he told himself. *Relax. Just answer.* "Not *on* it. I went around it once on a boat, but I was only about ten. I think it's a couple of miles long and mostly covered with bushes and trees."

For the next few minutes the boys were silent. Alex leaned out a little, enjoying the breeze and the occasional spray of water on his face. Then, as the boat slowed a little, he pointed ahead. "I think that's Loon Island. There's a boathouse at the end, anyway."

"I see it!" Jerry took another photo. "Well, I should get back to my family. Can I take your picture?" He held up his camera and took one before Alex could answer. Then, with a grin, he went back to stand with his parents, leaving Alex alone at the bow.

So he took my picture. Does that make me interesting or suspicious, in Jerry's book? The guy was strange, but he was also friendly. And it wasn't as if he and Jerry had to be real friends. Alex wouldn't see him again after this vacation.

"Alex!" his mom called. He hunched over the

railing and pretended not to hear her. She didn't call again, but Alex figured she wanted him to join her and his sisters.

Instead, he watched the rocky island tower out of the water like a fort. Steps, some carved into the rock and some made of wood, sloped steeply upward behind the boathouse. These merged into a path that led to a forest of evergreens and poplars. The trees formed a canopy, creating a long, black tunnel, like the entrance to a cave. It didn't look like a place Alex wanted to visit. It looked more like a place in which you might get lost, a place you should avoid.

* * *

By late afternoon, all the campers had left the boat with their luggage. Each family was directed to the small, single-room cabin assigned to them. Two giant rocks stood like soldiers by the cabin given to Alex and his family, one on each side of the path that led to the main lodge and dining room.

"They must have been left there by the glaciers," his mother explained. "No wonder they call this cabin Rocky Retreat."

Alex made a second trip back to the boathouse to get the rest of his family's bags. The trails still seemed threatening, so he hurried along them. He'd have to remember to take a flashlight with him in the evenings. He helped his mother empty the suitcases and put their clothes away on the open shelves.

The cabin was just a plain, wooden building with a pair of bunk beds and a few shelves. There were no chairs or table, no dresser, and no pictures on the wall.

"It's not very fancy," Alex said. "No wonder it's cheap."

"It's not that bad. Anyway, it's mostly for younger kids. Later in the season they hold regular camps here. That's why there are bunk beds."

His sisters, Lindsey and Beth, both wanted the top bunks, so Alex and his mother took the lower ones. Once they'd chosen their beds, they headed for dinner at the main lodge.

During dinner, Jerry came over with his camera to show Alex his recent pictures. Besides the ones from the boat, he had several from Kenora – a fisherman showing off his catch, a peeing dog, and a woman staring in the window of a souvenir shop. Alex didn't see why they were suspicious or interesting, but Jerry seemed excited about them.

After dinner everyone attended an info session with the camp director, Mrs. Barkley, a stout woman of about fifty. "Just call me Mrs. B," she told the group. She had lively eyes and wore her gray hair in a tight ponytail. Alex thought she looked friendly, but stern. That worried him. He hoped she didn't know who his family was, but she probably did. She'd told the campers that she was from Kenora and, sooner or later, everyone who lived there went to Simon's Steakhouse. And everyone gossiped about the waitresses. Anyway, if she *wasn't* suspicious of him – yeah, right – she would pity him. He had learned that most adults felt one way or the other toward him. He didn't like either.

Mrs. Barkley began by showing them a map of the island, pointing out the main features of the camp, the locations of facilities, and the beaches. Then she had everyone introduce themselves. There were eleven families, with one more expected to arrive in the morning. The group included a couple of little girls who seemed to be about five or six years old, which meant that he wouldn't have to worry about entertaining Lindsey and Beth over the vacation.

Alex wished he had left before the introductions. Mrs. Barkley didn't *say* anything, but when it was his turn, she gave him a sharp look. Yup, she knew who they were. Alex made a mental note to stay out of her way.

Mrs. Barkley explained the camp schedule and then offered to point out the hiking trails to everyone. Alex's mom left to take the girls to the washroom and Jerry's parents disappeared too. Only the two boys and some other adult campers stayed behind.

"There's a path on the west side of the island," Mrs. Barkley explained, her ponytail swinging as she looked between the map and the campers. "It's in rough shape because of the rocks and it's narrow, so it's not an easy hike."

"What about trails on the east side?" Jerry asked.

"There's a sort of trail part way, but it dies out. In the middle, here," she pointed, "there are a couple of short paths in from each side, but they don't connect." She looked at the two boys. Her eyes lingered on Alex, even though he hadn't said anything. "Be careful on the trails. I don't need you getting lost around here."

"We won't get lost," Alex said.

Jerry pointed at the bottom of the map. "What are those buildings at the south end?"

"There's an old fishing cabin and a couple of sheds down there. They've been deserted a long time and they're pretty run down. And the old pier isn't safe either. All of it's closed off to visitors.

Especially to kids." This time she looked directly at Alex. "I don't want any trouble from you boys," she added. Both of them nodded and Mrs. Barkley turned away to answer a question from another camper.

"What was all that about?" Jerry asked quietly as the boys left the lodge. "She was on your case and she doesn't even know you."

Alex shrugged. "What do I know? She's the one acting weird."

"Yeah, I guess so," Jerry said, but he looked disappointed by the answer. "I should have taken her picture. Do you think she'd let me?"

Alex couldn't help but laugh. "I dunno. She might bite off your head."

"Yeah, you're right. Hey, do you want to hike that trail tomorrow? The one on the west side? My dad says I should do more outdoors stuff. And who knows, when I get to be a detective, maybe I'll need to know my way around the woods."

"I thought you wanted to be a journalist."

"Yeah, that too. Do you want to go?"

Did he want to go? Alex wanted to hike, but he didn't know if he wanted to go with Jerry. He was used to going off and doing things on his own. This felt like a change that he wasn't ready for, but if he said no and Jerry saw him hiking tomorrow, then that would be awkward. "I guess so," he said.

Jerry said good-bye and Alex returned to his family's cabin. He was glad to get away from Mrs. Barkley's probing eyes, at least. When she looked at him, he felt as if she was trying to figure out what he was thinking. It was bad enough having his mother trying to read his mind. He didn't need someone else doing it too.

CHAPTER 2

ALEX WOKE WITH a start. A sharp, pattering sound had jarred him out of a deep sleep. He glanced around, but his mom and sisters still slept soundly. He was the only one awake.

Darn rain, Alex thought. The pattering stopped and then came again from a different section of the roof. That wasn't rain, Alex realized suddenly. Something – or someone – was making the noise.

The faint light streaming through the cabin window lit the face of his watch. It was five in the morning. He slipped out of bed, relieved that Lindsey and Beth had wanted the top bunks. He padded to the window and looked out. A thin mist hid the small beach below and obscured the surrounding trees, but he couldn't see any sign of rain.

The noise on the roof came again, louder this time. Then a rust-colored squirrel jumped off the roof and landed on the nearest rock. It scrambled up the overhanging branch of a spruce tree and disappeared. Was that what had woken him? His eyes searched the path, but he saw nothing but shadows.

Stop being so paranoid, Alex scolded himself. But that was useless. No matter how hard he tried to fight it, Loon Island gave him the creeps. Maybe it was the wisps of fog, or maybe the trees hanging over the paths. Maybe it was just something in the air.

He knew his family needed a break, especially his mother. Not long ago, she had taken on a couple of extra shifts to help cover their expenses. And now, on top of that, she wanted to try to "fix" him. Like he was broken or something.

Alex understood that his mom was worried and stressed out. He just didn't get how a holiday this close to home was going to help. Especially a holiday on an island in the Lake of the Woods. The lake was where his father had died. It was the place where his father had betrayed them.

And since the lake was the main attraction at Kenora, for tourists and residents, it was a part of Alex's life whether he wanted it to be or not. All he wanted was to leave the place behind. He wished they could just *move* somewhere else, period. Somewhere a thousand miles away from Kenora. Three years was a long time to live in a place where people still stared at you suspiciously when you passed by.

For a while his mother had tried selling the

house, but houses weren't selling well – what with all the layoffs at the paper mill. So they'd stayed put.

With a sigh, Alex crawled back under his still-warm blanket. He hoped he could fall back asleep, but it was too late – he was wide awake. That was when he decided not to hang out with Jerry anymore. *What's the point?* he thought. *I'm fine on my own.*

A crow cawed loudly several times, breaking into Alex's thoughts. He checked the time on his watch again – five-thirty. He was surprised his mother and sisters could sleep through the noise.

He silently slipped out of bed again. It was useless trying to sleep. He still wished he were somewhere else, but he might as well make the best of the situation.

He pulled on yesterday's clothes, taking care not to wake anyone. The screen door squeaked a little when he opened it, but nobody stirred.

Alex slid down the path to the lake below. It was steep. He tripped and skinned his knee, but he ignored the pain. Wisps of fog lifted off the water, looking like skeletal fingers. The sun was beginning to brighten the treetops. Before long the fog would burn away.

The lonely wail of a loon echoed somewhere out on the water. Another answered at a closer distance. *Pretty clear how this island gets its name*, Alex thought. A fish jumped, breaking the stillness of the calm water. The ripples circled out, then disappeared.

A narrow rim of beach bordered the northwest side of Loon Island. Sand had been deposited along a small section to cover some of the pebbles and stones. He walked past the sandy section, picked up a flat pebble, and tried to skip it across the water. The stone skipped once and sank.

He walked farther, occasionally turning over stones to search for crayfish. In one spot he smelled fish and found the remains of a dead muskie floating on the water.

A low whistle interrupted the quiet of the morning. Alex turned to see Jerry scrambling down the path behind the Wylies' cabin. Alex froze, feeling unsure what to do. He could just walk away, but that would be rude. He didn't exactly want to try and be friends with Jerry, but there was no way to avoid him.

"Looks like I'm not the only early bird," Jerry called to Alex. "Did that old crow wake you too?"

"I heard him," Alex said, "but it was a squirrel that woke me." He didn't say anything more. Maybe Jerry would get the hint and go away.

Alex looked down at Jerry's boots, which

looked brand-new.

Jerry followed Alex's gaze. "My new hiking boots. My dad insists I wear them while I'm here. He thinks they'll be good on the rocks."

"Better than my runners."

"Like I said, my dad's trying to get me more used to the outdoors – to toughen me up, he says." Jerry paused, and then said quickly, almost self-consciously, "He's really my stepfather. My parents divorced when I was two and Mom married this guy a few months ago. I just call him Dad because he likes that."

Alex didn't know what to say. He thought having two fathers must be better than having none.

"This is the first time I've worn the boots," Jerry went on, as if he wanted to get off the father topic.

"You better watch out for blisters then," Alex commented, feeling like he had to say something. He turned back to the beach and stared at the clearing fog.

"Do you want to do that hike we talked about?" Jerry suggested. "We could check out the west trail we saw last night on Mrs. B's map."

Alex sighed. Jerry was persistent. "OK, I guess." At least they wouldn't miss breakfast, which wasn't served until seven-thirty. They had nearly two hours to kill.

"Let me just go back to leave my parents a note. My mom's a real worrywart."

"OK," Alex said. "My mom's used to me going off on my own, so I didn't think of that." That wasn't exactly a lie. His mother *was* used to him going off on his own, but she didn't really like it.

Jerry hurried back to his cabin. He returned quickly, holding up a small canteen that he'd attached to his belt. "I brought some water."

"Good idea."

They started along the trail and discovered soon enough that Mrs. Barkley hadn't been kidding when she said it was in rough shape. Sharp stones jutted out of the ground unexpectedly. Alex could feel them through the thin soles of his shoes. He glanced enviously at Jerry's hiking boots, but said nothing. There was no way his mom could afford anything like that. Exposed roots snaked their way across the path and Jerry managed to trip over most of them. Alex had to agree with Jerry's dad – Jerry could use some more experience in the outdoors.

"Water break," Alex suggested after a while. They sat on a couple of rocks, located where the trail divided, and shared a drink. Jerry snapped a photo of Alex and another of the canteen lying on the rock.

"Maybe we've gone far enough this way," said Jerry. "Besides, Mrs. B said we shouldn't go too far on this trail, and ..."

"What Mrs. Barkley doesn't know won't hurt her," Alex said. "And it's still too early for breakfast."

"Let's take this other trail then." Jerry pointed inland, away from the lake.

Alex shrugged. "OK. It doesn't matter to me. Maybe it connects to the other side."

The new trail wasn't as stony, but it was narrow. "I think it's more of a deer path," Alex said, but he led them along it. Each time Alex pushed through a clump of bushes, branches snapped back like elastics. Jerry followed at a distance to avoid getting hit in the face. The path seemed to go nowhere, so Alex was about to suggest turning around. But then the trail opened into a small clearing about fifty yards across. In the center of the clearing stood a single spruce tree. And beside it was a heap of fresh dirt.

"What's that?" asked Jerry, panting slightly. He pulled out his camera. "Has someone been digging here?'

"Probably just an animal," Alex said. "A groundhog or something."

Jerry hurried across the clearing and knelt

beside the dirt pile. He pointed to a distinct footprint in the soil. "It wasn't an animal," he said. "That's human." He stood up and measured his own shoe to the print. "It must be a man's track. It's bigger than mine." He rubbed his chin thoughtfully and pretended to look surprised. "A mystery, my friend."

Alex rolled his eyes. "It's probably just a hiker from Family Camp."

"But the place just opened for the season. Mrs. B said so." Jerry paused as if to make a dramatic statement. "So that means it could be a trespasser, right?" He moved closer to the pile and snapped a couple of photos.

"Maybe you've just been watching too much TV," Alex said. Still, he had to admit Jerry did have a point.

"That's what my dad says. But see, there are shovel marks," he added. "And more footprints." He knelt beside the hole and examined it with an imaginary magnifying glass.

Alex edged up beside him and peered into the hole.

"Hey, stay off the dirt," Jerry warned. "We don't want to leave our footprints too."

"Relax, Sherlock," Alex said, but he quickly stepped back again. "So why would someone dig out here in the middle of nowhere?"

"Somebody's digging for gold," Jerry joked. "Buried treasure – or Spanish doubloons – or precious jewels!"

"Don't get too excited," Alex broke in. "There's no gold on any of these islands. And no buried treasure either."

"Should we tell someone?" asked Jerry. Then he shrugged. "I guess there's no law against digging a hole."

"I suppose not. Unless ... hey, it couldn't be a grave, could it?"

"It's only about three feet deep and it's too round."

"Yeah, you're right."

The boys searched around the clearing but nothing else stood out. Only the trees leaned menacingly above them and a slight breeze made the leaves shiver.

"Let's go," suggested Jerry. "Breakfast should be ready soon and I'm starved."

"Me too," Alex said.

On the walk back, Alex remained silent, trying not to be paranoid about the hole. Jerry wasn't helping, though. He kept coming up with all sorts of fantastic explanations.

Alex finally got a break when Jerry went to join

his family for breakfast.

Relax, he told himself. But it was hard to. Why did the Lake of the Woods need to have so many secrets? It was as if the place was haunting him.

CHAPTER 3

THE NEXT MORNING, over a big breakfast in the dining hall, Mr. Wylie suggested that Alex and Jerry take a small fishing trip with him. "No use wasting our week here," he said. "And the weather looks great today."

Alex was going to pass on the offer. He'd planned to hike down the west side of the island and check out the hole again – alone this time. Fishing with Jerry and his bossy stepdad didn't sound like a whole lot of fun. And he didn't really like boats anymore.

But his mother overheard Mr. Wylie asking him to join them and she butted in to accept. There was no polite way to refuse now.

"The girls and I will go to the beach," she said. "You go ahead with your new friend. Have some fun. Just be sure to wear a life jacket."

"Yeah, yeah," Alex said. "I *can* swim you know." But he knew that wasn't why she was afraid. His father had known how to swim too.

"Which boat will we take?" asked Jerry as he, his father, and Alex walked down the steps to the boathouse.

Mr. Wylie stopped halfway down. "We're taking a canoe, not a boat. I don't have my operator card to run a motorboat."

That was fine with Alex. Canoes didn't give him the same bad feeling as boats did. But disappointment showed on Jerry's face. "Does that matter, Dad?" he asked.

"It's the law. Besides, I prefer canoes. They make you work a little instead of just sitting there. And they're not as noisy. I like the silence as they glide through the water – makes me feel like a fur trader from a hundred years ago." He paused. "A little exercise with a paddle won't hurt you, son."

"But aren't motorboats safer than canoes?" Jerry persisted. "On TV they say ..."

"You watch too much TV. I've told you that before. Canoes are fine, if you're careful. Motor-boats go too fast anyway."

Mr. Wylie stopped beside the four canoes tied to the pier. "Mrs. B said to take the yellow one and to find life jackets inside the boathouse. Why don't you boys go fetch some for all of us? I'll study the map here and try to figure out a few good places to fish."

"OK, OK," Jerry muttered. The boys went inside the boathouse. It was small, but crammed with paddles, oars, and life jackets in various sizes and colors. Keys for the boats hung on nails just inside the door.

"I guess they have enough life jackets from when they have their regular kids' camps," said Alex as they sorted through the pile. He grabbed a red one to try for size.

"Has anyone ever gotten lost around here?" Jerry asked as he reached for an orange jacket.

The question took Alex by surprise. He glanced quickly at Jerry. It was almost as if Jerry knew more than he was letting on.

Jerry, however, was concentrating on tying the life jacket. If anything, he looked more nervous than Alex.

Alex swallowed hard. "Yeah, I heard about someone once. But it was a long time ago."

"What happened? Did the person make it?" Now Jerry sounded a little freaked out.

Alex chose his words carefully. "It was at the south end of the lake, miles from here. And someone found him after a day or two. But like I said, it was a long time ago. I wasn't very old. I don't remember the details."

"Mrs. B would probably know," Jerry said. "Maybe I should go ask her."

"Don't ask her!" Alex snapped. Then, seeing the startled look on Jerry's face, he added, "You saw how crabby she was. She'd probably snarl at you for bothering her."

Jerry frowned. "You're the touchy one! And it was you she was crabby with, not me."

"Sorry," Alex said. "Look, it's all ancient history. And don't worry, *we* won't get lost. To make sure, we'll check out that map with your dad."

"I guess," Jerry muttered. "We probably won't get far in a canoe anyway." He followed Alex to the large map nailed on the outside wall of the boathouse.

"You probably know all about using a canoe, don't you?" Jerry said with a trace of envy. They climbed gingerly into the yellow canoe, while Mr. Wylie steadied it.

"A little," Alex answered. "But I'm sort of out of practice. We took lessons in gym class."

"You can give Jerry some paddling tips, Alex," suggested Mr. Wylie as he stowed his tackle box and the sandwiches the cook had provided. "He can use a little help." He handed Alex the rods to keep at the front.

Alex nodded, but he noticed Jerry's red face and didn't say anything.

They set off with Alex at the bow, Jerry in the middle, and Mr. Wylie at the back.

"Let's head south along the west shore first,"

suggested Mr. Wylie. "Then we can come back on the east side and stop to fish. Mrs. Barkley said there was a good spot along there."

At first, their paddling was rather jerky, especially Jerry's. Every time he lifted his paddle out of the lake, he splashed water onto Alex's back. Mr. Wylie finally noticed and suggested that Jerry paddle on the other side. "And try to keep time with Alex's stroke. I'll change sides as needed, to steer."

Before long they all got into a rhythm and the canoe glided through the calm water. Drops of water ran off the paddles, sparkling in the sunlight.

The trees nearly reached the shore along most of the west side, though there were a few open spots. A narrow band of sand and gravel edged the island, like a white fringe on a dark green tablecloth. Here and there Alex glimpsed the trail he and Jerry had followed yesterday. The path looked easier to travel when seen from the water – from this distance you couldn't see all the rocks and roots jutting out of the ground.

"That must be the old cabin," Alex announced when they rounded the southwest tip of the island and saw several deserted buildings ahead. "Are you taking a picture, Jerry?"

"I didn't bring my camera," he answered

regretfully. "I was afraid it might get wet."

"You guys want to stop here?" suggested Mr. Wylie. Alex remembered that Jerry's father hadn't been there when Mrs. Barkley told them to stay away from the cabin.

"Maybe," Alex said, hesitating. If he said yes, and Mrs. Barkley found out, he would be in trouble.

"We shouldn't," Jerry said suddenly. "Mrs. B said ..."

"She said to be careful," Alex cut him off. He didn't want to get in trouble, but he also didn't want to lose the chance to explore the area another time. "Because the pier and buildings are so old," he added.

Jerry looked confused, but he caught on and didn't say another word.

"They do look old," Mr. Wylie agreed. "If you do go, stay off the pier and don't go inside the buildings."

They paddled around the southeast corner and started north along the east side. Here there was no fringe of sand at all. Spruce, pine, birch, and poplars crowded down to the shore. The bank was steep in many places. Often the roots of trees hung over the edge, exposed to wind and waves. They looked like bony brown hands holding on for dear life to the rugged shoreline. The wind had twisted the trees into weird shapes, and branches from different trees had locked together, forming a natural gate.

Alex glanced back once in a while at Jerry and Mr. Wylie. He felt a twinge of envy when Mr. Wylie teased Jerry by playfully splashing water on him with his paddle. Alex felt like an outsider.

"Looks like a small creek ahead," he called back from the bow. "Is that where Mrs. Barkley said we should fish?"

"I think so," Mr. Wylie said. "The mouth of a creek is usually a good spot."

"What kinds of fish can we catch?" Jerry asked as Mr. Wylie back paddled to stop the canoe. Alex reached for his rod, but Jerry was holding his hands up in a square, pretending to frame a picture.

"You name it," said Alex. "The tourist books say pickerel, pike, perch, bass, muskies." He glanced back at Mr. Wylie. "Do we have bait?"

"I've got night crawlers. And these spoons and jigs." Mr. Wiley opened his tackle box and handed out hooks. "Let's start with these. Come on, Jerry. Grab a rod."

Soon all three rods were in action. The canoe was crowded and lines flew dangerously in every direction.

"Watch out!" Mr. Wylie growled when Jerry's

hook just missed his ear. Then he snagged his own hook on a branch that stuck out from the shore.

Alex wasn't any better. Twice he tangled his line with Jerry's. He'd just unsnarled it for the second time when Jerry dropped his rod in the water.

"My rod!" Jerry yelled, leaning out to grab it. The canoe tipped to the right. Alex swung his weight the other way and the canoe rocked left.

"Stop it!" screamed Jerry. "I can't swim, you know!" He seemed to have forgotten he was wearing a life jacket.

"Take it easy. Take it easy," Mr. Wylie said. "Keep calm, boys. Settle down."

Both boys stopped moving and the rocking of the canoe slowly eased. "Sorry," Jerry muttered as he tossed his wet rod into the bottom of the canoe.

"My fault too," said Alex. He took a deep breath, trying to slow his heartbeat. "I think I need a break. Can Jerry and I go ashore and explore for a bit?" Jerry gave him a startled look but didn't say anything.

"Good idea," agreed Mr. Wylie. "Three fishermen in a canoe is two too many. Reel in your lines," he said as he turned the canoe to shore.

There was a small inlet where the creek entered the lake and where the banks were not so steep. It wasn't hard to land the canoe so the boys could climb out. "Stretch your legs a little," said Mr. Wylie. "But don't go too far. Stay within earshot. And put on some more sun block, both of you." He tossed the bottle to Jerry.

After dropping their life jackets on the beach, Alex and Jerry did as he said. Then they pushed through a thick stand of poplars. The creek was nothing but a trickle between the low banks. Branches intertwined above the water.

"What's up?" asked Jerry. "Why did you want to get out here?"

Alex shrugged. "I was just bored," he said. He didn't want to explain that sometimes water made him uneasy too – even though he knew how to swim. "Plus I want to check out that hole again," he added.

"You think this is the way?"

"It's the only creek we've seen so far," said Alex. "And there was a creek running out of the clearing, remember?"

"Hey, you're right. I should have thought of that ... but we'd better stick close to the creek or we'll wind up lost.

Alex bent down under a branch overhanging the water. Then he pointed to the creek bed. "See? This is the way. Someone walked here recently. Whoever dug the hole came in this way."

"Good thinking," said Jerry. "You should be a detective too!"

After following the creek for a few minutes, the boys arrived at the clearing. Alex stopped at the edge and waited for Jerry to catch up. "Look," he whispered, pointing ahead.

Both boys stared. Where yesterday there had been one hole and one pile of dirt, today there were two – on opposite sides of the spruce tree. The smell of freshly dug earth lingered in the air.

Alex chewed on his lip. He didn't know what it meant, but the presence of a second hole creeped him out.

Jerry backed nervously into the bush. "Maybe we should go back to the canoe."

"Just a minute," Alex said, trying to sound braver than he felt. "Let's have a look around." He parted the bushes and walked across the clearing to the new hole. Jerry didn't move.

Suddenly Alex stopped. In the new pile of dirt, something shiny caught his eye. He stooped to examine it, then dropped to one knee. It was a medallion. Alex's heart pounded loudly in his ears. The medallion was identical to the one his father – his dead father – used to wear around his neck. Keeping his back to Jerry, he picked it up and thrust it into his pocket.

"You find something?" Jerry called.

"N ... no," Alex stammered, his brain spinning feverishly. What was this medallion doing here?

"Aw, come on," Jerry coaxed as he came across the clearing. "I saw you put something in your pocket. What is it?"

Alex took a deep breath, trying to overcome his sudden fear. "Not much, really – sort of a medallion thing, I guess." He pulled from his pocket the small, shiny badge. He held it out briefly and then shoved it back.

"Let me look," Jerry said, holding out his hand. "Whoever was digging here must have dropped it."

Alex hesitated, then handed the medallion over. It was a silver oval, about two inches in diameter, decorated with scrolls and circles. There was a small broken loop on the top.

"Looks like it was hanging on a chain and broke off," Jerry said. Then he turned it over. "What's this on the back?"

Alex pretended to look. "Letters, I guess," he said. "They're kind of scratched off."

Jerry turned it carefully toward the sun. "Letters, all right. I can still read them, I think." He peered closely. "Looks like C.O. to me. See what you think."

"C.O.? Are you sure?" Alex moved forward to

examine it more closely. His father's initials were S.O. – S for Steven, O for O'Grady. C.O. were his uncle's initials. But his uncle was in prison, where he'd been for nearly three years ... at least he was supposed to be. *Other people could have a medallion like this. It could be anyone's.*

But with those initials, Alex? That's too much of a coincidence.

"I wish I had my camera," said Jerry. He handed the medallion back and Alex stuck it quickly into his pocket.

"Let's get going," Alex said. "Your dad's probably waiting for us. And I've had enough of this place." He needed to get away from the clearing so he could think things through.

"Not yet," said Jerry. "You've got *me* curious now. Let's look around a bit more." He glanced at Alex, who was chewing on his lip again. "Is something wrong? Are you OK?"

"Nothing's wrong," Alex snapped. "This place is giving me the creeps, that's all."

"You're right," Jerry admitted. "It's awfully quiet around here – too quiet! Just let me look around for a couple of minutes to see if there's anything else suspicious."

He took a few more turns around the clearing while Alex watched. The more Jerry looked around, the more anxious Alex became. "Let's go," he urged.

"All right, all right," Jerry muttered.

The boys started back down the creek. The trees closed in around them, shutting out the sunlight.

CHAPTER 4

"**ARE YOU GAME** for another hike?" Jerry asked
Alex over breakfast the next morning.

Alex's heart sank. He *had* been planning a hike
– but he'd wanted to go alone. He needed to solve
the mystery of the medallion, but if Jerry came
along, he would have to hide what he was trying to
do. "I suppose so," he said. "But I want to go all
the way down the west side."

Jerry looked doubtful. "That wasn't my plan
but I guess ..."

"You don't have to go," Alex said quickly.

"No, I'll go. Meet me at my cabin in ten
minutes, OK?" Jerry scurried off to get ready.

Mrs. Wylie was stuffing granola bars into Jerry's
pocket when Alex got there. "Be careful you don't
get lost," she warned. "I'm not sure I like you two
hiking off on your own. Even if it is a small island."

"They'll be fine, Myrna," Mr. Wylie reassured
her. "Don't get your shirt in a knot. Exploring is
good for boys."

"We'll be careful," Jerry promised his mother.
"Alex knows how to figure out directions from
the trees. The thickest moss grows on the north

side, right?"

"Right," Alex agreed. "Most of the time. But with the sun shining, it's easy to figure out directions."

With a wave, the two started off, but they'd barely gone a hundred yards when Mr. Wylie caught up to them. "Take this whistle your mother brought. If you get lost, blow it to help us locate you. And make sure the two of you stay together."

"Sure, sure," Jerry muttered, shoving the whistle into his pocket.

"He's a bit of a worrywart, too, isn't he?" said Alex, once they were out of earshot. "Or maybe he's just humoring your mother." He'd forgotten how protective his own dad used to be when it came to his children. That was ironic, considering what his father had done. Anger curdled in his stomach.

"I heard something last night," Jerry said, breaking into Alex's thoughts. "My parents were talking after they thought I was asleep."

"Talking about what?"

"Mrs. B told them that people have seen lights at night on some of the islands. Not this one, but two or three islands over by the Devil's Gap."

"What kind of lights?" asked Alex. "Fires? Flashlights? Or what?"

"I dunno. They didn't really say. Just that it's

been going on for a week or two and the lights seem to move around."

"So what did Mrs. Barkley think it was?" Alex still couldn't bring himself to call her Mrs. B.

"Mom and Dad didn't say." Jerry paused and then added with a grin, "If it's over by the Devil's Gap, it could be ghosts. Those dead warriors you told me about."

"Here we go again," Alex said. "Too much TV." *So that's why Jerry wants to explore today*, he thought. But now Alex felt hesitant to go. Stories of strange happenings on the lake reminded him of three years ago, about things he'd sooner forget. It was as if the lake were cursed.

"If you remember," he added sharply, "I also told you it was probably just a legend, made up to bring tourists out here."

"Maybe so," Jerry said with a shrug. "But people *have* been seeing lights at night." He stayed silent for a moment, then added, "Maybe we should tell somebody about the holes we found."

"No!" Alex snapped. If the holes had something to do with his father or uncle, he wanted to be the first to know. Then, realizing how forceful he sounded, he softened his voice. "The holes aren't that big a deal. Rock hounds probably made them. I heard someone say they come on these islands."

"Maybe. But what if there's a connection? Between the lights and the holes we found, I mean. We could tell someone and ask them about the strange lights."

"You aren't supposed to know about those lights, remember?" Alex paused, not sure how else he could convince Jerry not to tell anyone about the holes.

"Maybe ..."

"Relax, Sherlock." Alex tried to grin. *I need to get Jerry's mind onto something else*, he thought. *Before he brings up the medallion again*. "Let's just forget the holes," he added. "I want to explore those buildings we saw from the canoe."

"At the south end?" Jerry stopped walking. "But Mrs. B said they were off limits."

"We can just look," said Alex.

"I guess ... as long as we don't get in trouble." Then he smirked a little and started along the trail again. "My dad did ask us yesterday if we wanted to stop there. And he does want me to toughen up. So in a way, I am allowed to break a few rules."

"So let's try it."

The trail seemed easier this time. Jerry didn't trip so often and they were able to move faster than before. *I guess we're both getting used to it*, Alex thought. After a while they passed the turnoff they'd taken the first morning – the trail that took them to the clearing with the first hole. Alex didn't mention it and Jerry didn't seem to notice they had passed it. Alex was relieved – he wanted to explore the cabin.

A few minutes later, Alex scrambled past a large rock into a clearing that was larger than the one that had the holes. "We're here," he announced when Jerry caught up.

The buildings, at first glance, didn't look like much. The cabin was small and its logs weather beaten. The only window was now a gaping hole and the door sagged open. Two sheds, both a dull gray-brown, stood next to the cabin. Their doors hung on rusty hinges and one of the sheds had a hole in its roof.

"Wanna have a peek?" asked Jerry. He walked up to the cabin and peered through the half-open door. He seemed a lot more confident now about breaking the rules.

Alex hesitated. The cabin looked like it might fall down on them as soon as they entered.

"Maybe we shouldn't go *in*," he said.

"I didn't say to go *in*. Just to *look*." Jerry took another step and then stopped. "How come there's no dust?" He headed for the sheds. Then, leaning over, he peeked inside the first door before moving on to the next.

Alex watched him with a puzzled expression. "What are you doing?"

Jerry frowned. "There's something a little strange here." He knelt at the doorway of one of the sheds and ran his finger through the thick layer of dust that carpeted the entrance. Then he moved to the second shed and did it again.

"Hey," Alex said. "What's up?"

Jerry shrugged and returned to the old cabin. "Look," he said. "There's a layer of dust and dirt and old leaves inside those sheds. How come there's no dust or leaves and junk in the entrance of the cabin?" He tried to peer inside the window, then stepped back again and examined the doorway. "It almost looks as if it's been swept out or something. Come and look."

Alex peeked through the doorway. "Yeah, you're right. But so what?"

Jerry stepped through the sagging door and Alex followed somewhat reluctantly. The cabin had a dusty smell, kind of like mildew. A dull light streamed through the dirty windows and door. In the dimness, they could see that someone had been at work cleaning up the grime.

As their eyes grew accustomed to the gloomy interior, Jerry pointed at something. "Hey, what's that in the corner?"

Alex edged closer and then bent down. "Looks like a sleeping bag all rolled up." He picked it up and turned it toward the light. "It looks brand new. Still has the tags on it." He turned to Jerry. "What do you suppose it's doing here –" he smirked "– Sherlock?"

"I'd say someone is using this cabin to sleep," Jerry suggested. "And recently too." Then he shivered. "Let's get out of here. Now I'm the one getting the creeps!"

"Scared?" Alex grinned at him, though he wasn't at ease either. He placed the bag back in the same spot and hurried out after Jerry. "Whoever is using this cabin isn't here now, anyway – I hope."

He scanned the clearing while he spoke, but didn't see anything unusual. There were too many mysteries on this lake. He was already wondering if the sleeping bag was connected to the holes and the medallion.

"Let's look at the old pier while we're here," Jerry suggested. He grinned. "My dad would say I'm in full detective mode now."

Alex didn't hesitate. He was too curious. Anyway, Mrs. Barkley would never find out that they had broken her rules. He followed Jerry to the edge of the lake.

The dock *was* in bad shape. The rotting boards were littered with holes larger than Alex's hand. One whole plank was missing and he stepped gingerly over the gap. There was an ominous creaking sound.

"Be careful!" Jerry warned. "The whole thing might give way."

Alex knelt at the far end of the pier and examined the supporting posts to be sure it would hold up. It looked as if it could collapse at any time. "Don't come too close," he said. "But see this? I think something was tied up here. These look like fresh scrape marks, like a boat or canoe has rubbed against it."

"And look there," said Jerry. "Looks like a fresh sliver of wood is missing from that board. It's a lighter color here, not as faded as the rest of the boards."

"Maybe somebody just stopped here for a moment," Alex suggested. "You can't really tell how recent ..." He stopped abruptly. Somewhere in the distance the dull roar of a motor sounded.

"Is someone coming?" Alex asked. The roar grew louder and his heart picked up speed. "Let's get out of here."

Jerry didn't have to be told twice. Both boys dashed across the pier. It swayed dangerously and

Alex felt a board start to give way beneath his foot. He leaped the last few feet to shore, then followed Jerry across the opening and up the trail.

"Get behind that rock," Alex panted. Both boys fell to their knees behind it and peered at the lake through a tangle of branches.

A motorboat loaded with four khaki-clad men sped past the pier without stopping. "Just fishermen," Alex said.

Jerry grinned wryly. "Nothing to worry about."

"No," Alex agreed, "but that was close. We should head back anyway. Your mom will have a fit if we're gone much longer."

"But what's going on here?" asked Jerry as they started up the trail. "Weird holes. A sleeping bag in a cabin that's off limits and falling apart. Someone using a pier that's not safe to use anymore. Isn't it all weird?"

Alex shrugged. He was starting to have his own suspicions, but he didn't want to share them with Jerry.

"Doesn't Family Camp own all of Loon Island?" Jerry persisted.

"I think so."

"Then we should tell Mrs. B what we've found. Whatever's going on here might be illegal."

"We can't tell Mrs. Barkley!" Alex said.

"Remember, she told us to keep away from these buildings."

"But somebody's been trespassing here and digging the holes we saw yesterday and ..."

"That could mean anything. For all we know, maybe Mrs. Barkley hired somebody as a watchman to sleep here. But if she finds out we've been here, then *we'll* be in trouble!" said Alex. "We'll be grounded. Or worse."

"She wouldn't kick us out of camp, would she?"

"Who knows? Anyway, it's nothing to do with us. It could just be a fisherman who stopped for the night and forgot his bag. And the holes are nothing but holes."

"Maybe," Jerry agreed, wrinkling his forehead. Then he grinned. "But I'm in detective mode. And really, why would somebody leave a brand-new sleeping bag in a dump like that?"

"Search me," Alex answered. "But it's none of our business. So let's not mention what we found. OK?"

"Yeah, yeah, OK. There just seems to be a lot happening on this island, that's all. What if there's something –" he struggled for the right word "– something criminal, going on here, like I was saying?"

"It's not against the law to dig holes or leave

sleeping bags behind." Alex tried to sound casual, then added with a grin, "Relax ... let's just forget it and head back to the lodge. It's getting hot."

They began walking again, but Alex couldn't ease the turmoil in his mind. Jerry wasn't far off the mark – if his uncle *was* involved, then something criminal probably was going on at the island. He needed to find some time alone, as soon as possible, to think things through.

* * *

Alex crouched under the shelter of a giant spruce, not far from the rear of the main lodge. From here he could easily watch the campers as they gathered for a wiener roast and a sing-along. Mrs. Barkley was herding everyone together, but Alex had no desire to join them. As long as he stayed still under the spruce branches, nobody would see him, even if someone came looking.

He'd heard his mother calling out for him about fifteen minutes ago. Soon he'd have to join the group around the fire. Besides, he didn't really want to miss the hot dogs, though he could do without the singing. But before that, he needed to be alone for a little while.

He caught sight of the leaping flames of the

bonfire through the trees. As the twilight faded, the flames brightened against the sky. The near full moon was beginning to make shadows, but Alex found them comforting.

"Did you show anyone the medallion?" Jerry had asked as they left the lodge after dinner. Alex, startled by the abrupt question, said the first thing that came to mind.

"No. And, anyway, I think I lost it. I've got a hole in my pocket, and it's gone. So let's forget I ever found the dumb thing."

"Really," said Jerry, raising his eyebrows. He eyed Alex suspiciously. "Well, that's too bad. I wanted to take a picture of it. If you *find* it," he paused dramatically, "let me know." Jerry hadn't accused Alex of lying, but he might as well have.

So now I've got Jerry mad at me, Alex thought. He tried not to let it bother him. He was used to the cold shoulder by now.

Alex *had* considered showing the medallion to his mother. But something stopped him. Three years ago, his mother had a really hard time getting over what Alex's father had done. Like Alex, she hadn't know whom to blame. Eventually she'd stopped being angry and that's what she wanted Alex to do too. But seeing the medallion would just reopen old wounds.

Alex closed his eyes. He wanted to stop reliving the past, but it seemed impossible. No matter what he did, the past thrust itself back into his face. Like when he walked down the streets at home and parents stared at him suspiciously. Or when he tried to make friends with a new girl in school and she stopped talking to him after learning who he was.

But what was the medallion doing here, of all places? Obviously, it hadn't been at Loon Island for long, because the silver was untarnished. But Uncle Carl was in prison. Could someone else have taken the medallion and dropped it off here? Was someone playing a prank or was something more dangerous going on?

As for showing it to Mrs. Barkley, no way! If he started talking about mysterious holes and lost sleeping bags, she would accuse him of trying to cause trouble. She would probably think *he* was the one responsible. *Like father, like son* – that's what everyone thought.

He just hoped Jerry wouldn't remember to ask her about anyone getting lost on the Lake of the Woods.

Alex crawled out from under the protection of the big spruce. He might as well join the others at the campfire. The shadows no longer seemed comforting.

Thinking things through hadn't really helped. The holes and the medallion and the sleeping bag had to mean something. But what? How they were connected, if at all? The only choice he had was to visit both places again to look for more clues.

CHAPTER 5

THE CABIN WAS just beginning to lighten when Alex woke up. His internal alarm clock had worked, the way it usually did at home. He pulled on the clothes he had placed near his bed and tiptoed silently out of the cabin. He wished he had hiking boots like Jerry's, but his sneakers would have to do.

Thick fog hung over Loon Island, hiding the neighboring islands and most of the lake. A slight breeze swirled the fog and wet mist dampened Alex's face as he took the path to Jerry's cabin.

Last night Alex had decided to invite Jerry to hike with him to the south end of the island. He preferred to go alone, but he still felt bad about lying. It was the only peace offering Alex could think of.

Jerry had accepted right away, surprisingly, and he didn't even seem annoyed. But there was no movement at the Wylie cabin now. Jerry was nowhere in sight.

Alex waited for a few minutes, growing impatient and a little cold from standing still for so long. If they didn't start soon, it would be too late to go to the south end and get back before breakfast. He didn't want everyone knowing where they had been.

Alex picked up a few pebbles from the path and tossed them at the window he knew was closest to Jerry's bed. He waited, then tossed a few more. Suddenly Jerry's face appeared behind the glass and just as suddenly it disappeared. A few seconds later Jerry slipped out the door, carrying his boots and a strange, double-billed, green plaid cap.

"Sorry," Jerry whispered, sitting on a rock to do up his boots. "I thought that noisy crow would wake me like he did the last two mornings. Guess he doesn't like the fog." He pulled two hotdogs from his jacket pocket and handed one to Alex. "Here. I saved these from last night. They're a bit squashed and they're cold, but it's food."

"Thanks. What's with the hat?"

Jerry grinned. "This is my detective cap. I found it at a garage sale. I like to wear it when I'm investigating things."

"Looks weird, if you ask me!"

"Did I ask you? I brought a magnifying glass too."

Alex shrugged. If Jerry wanted to act like a nerdy detective, that was up to him. "Come on, then, let's move it!"

They set off, munching on the cold dogs as

they walked. The mist made the rocks slippery and they walked slowly, stepping carefully over stray stones and snaking roots.

Alex pointed out a large, brown-capped mushroom under a tree. "Did you bring your camera? Maybe that would be something for your collection."

"Darn!" Jerry slapped his forehead. "I was in such a rush I forgot it. And I forgot to leave my mom a note too. She won't be happy if she wakes up before I get back."

Alex shrugged. He wasn't going to turn back now. "We'll be back soon enough," he said. "She won't even know you're gone."

The closer they got to the south end of the island, the thicker the fog became. Jerry, trailing behind Alex, became a ghostly shape, barely visible in the swirling mist.

"We could get lost in this," he called up to Alex. His voice seemed to come out of nowhere.

"I think we're nearly there," Alex reassured him. He didn't like the feeling of being engulfed by the fog. The stillness was unnerving. There were no singing birds and even the squirrels seemed to be asleep. The only sound was the lonesome calls of the loons.

A large rock loomed up ahead and Alex

remembered that it marked the end of the trail. He turned to call back, just in time to see Jerry's silhouette tremble and then fall heavily toward the ground.

"You all right?" He went back to help Jerry up.

"I think so," Jerry began, but when he stood and put weight on his left foot, he groaned. "I must have sprained it a little."

"Can you walk? We're at the end of the trail."

"I'll try." He leaned on Alex and hobbled ahead to the rock. Then, wincing, he lowered himself carefully. "Just let me rest for a few minutes."

Alex waited beside him, feeling disappointed. With Jerry hurt, he wouldn't have enough time to examine the cabin, the sheds, or the old wharf. He felt irritated at Jerry for his clumsiness and then guilty for feeling that way.

"If you can't walk, I'll hike back for help," he said. "Your dad could get someone to bring a boat here."

"It's too wet and cold to sit in one place for long," Jerry said with a grimace. "And I don't want to wait by that cabin alone."

The gray-brown walls of the cabin and the sheds, though they were close by, melted into the swirling fog. The lake was practically hidden from view and the old wharf was only a darker shadow out in the grayness.

"Let me check around a little first," suggested Alex. Perhaps he could still accomplish what he'd come for.

"OK," said Jerry. "You be the detective. Here, take my hat."

Alex rolled his eyes but decided to indulge him. He pulled the plaid cap down over his ears, as if to show he meant business. Leaving Jerry on the rock, he crossed the clearing to the two sheds. A quick glance there showed him that the dust in the sheds was undisturbed, but it was the cabin that concerned him most.

He stopped by the window, trying to peek in, but couldn't see a thing. A chill ran down his spine as he peered into the dark interior. A minute ago he'd been joking with Jerry about detective work, but it didn't seem so funny now.

Maybe they should just start back. If Alex supported Jerry, or found him a walking stick, they could make it back to Family Camp.

Dragging his feet, Alex moved to the gaping doorway. He still saw nothing. The fog outside made the inside look darker than the last time they were here. Alex wished he had thought to bring a flashlight. He shivered.

"Hey, Alex! Are you almost done? I think my

ankle's swelling." Jerry's voice sounded faint in the fog, as if he were much farther away than he was.

Alex didn't answer. It would only take him one minute to look inside and then he would turn back. He pulled the cap low over his forehead, took a deep breath, and stepped through the doorway. At first he could see nothing. Then, as his eyes adjusted to the dim light, he made out what looked to be two boxes stacked in the middle of the floor.

He gulped. Somebody *had* been here since the last time! His eyes darted to the far corner, where they'd seen the brown sleeping bag. Instead of the sleeping bag he saw a lump of some kind. That was when he heard the faint sound of another person breathing – someone else was in the cabin with him.

He took another deep breath. That stale hot dog was no longer sitting well in his stomach.

He turned to run, took one stride and then, with a crash, tripped over something metal and fell to the floor.

The lump lengthened and leapt up. "Who's there?"

Alex held his breath and didn't move. Maybe the man wouldn't see him. Maybe ...

But the man, swearing loudly, freed himself from his sleeping bag and stumbled toward him. Alex pushed aside the shovel he'd tripped over and dashed for the doorway. He was too slow. A steely grip closed over his shoulder.

"Hold it, kid!" a deep voice growled, and he was pulled roughly back into the cabin. "What are you doing snooping around here?"

Alex fought to control his terror. There was no reason to think he was in danger ... but that's how he felt anyway. "I ... I was ... just exploring," he managed to stutter. "You scared me, that's all. That's why I ran."

"Exploring in this fog? At this hour of the morning?"

"I ... I don't know. We got lost," Alex answered, still trying to catch his breath and hide his fear. He couldn't see the man's face in the darkness of the cabin, but the gravelly voice sounded familiar.

"We?" the man hissed in a low voice. "Who else is with you?"

Alex hesitated. Should he scream? Try to trip the man and break his grip? Grab the shovel and hit him over the head?

"Well?" the man demanded more urgently, tightening his hold. As if to loosen his tongue, he gave Alex a hard shake.

"I ... I was with a friend, but he hurt his ankle. Way back on the trail. So he headed back to the camp." Alex felt a new sense of confidence with this lie. "This is Loon Island, you know. The camp owns the whole island."

"That so!" the voice hardened. "You saying I shouldn't be here?"

Alex gulped, his newfound confidence evaporating. "Uh, no, I ... I didn't say that."

"But that's what you meant." There was a pause and then the man continued, as if talking to himself. "And what am I going to do with you now? One more night that's – all I needed. I don't need a lousy kid nosing around."

Alex listened carefully. He was still not able to make out the man's face. Then, with a start, he realized he didn't need to see him. He recognized that voice.

CHAPTER 6

ALEX FELT SICK. The cold dog he'd eaten an hour ago lurched again in the pit of his stomach. At the same time he felt as if someone had squeezed all the air out of his lungs. The anger and sorrow he'd felt three years ago rushed back. The man who had grabbed him was his uncle.

He opened his mouth to shout – to say that he recognized the man   then closed it again just as quickly. Perhaps it was better not to say anything. If Uncle Carl believed Alex was some ignorant kid from Family Camp, maybe he'd just let him go – maybe. After discovering what his uncle was capable of three years ago, Alex didn't know how far he might go now.

Uncle Carl pulled Alex to the corner where he'd been sleeping. Alex was too shocked to try and struggle. Uncle Carl held him easily with one arm while he fumbled around on the cabin floor. He switched on a flashlight, revealing the sleeping bag, a pile of tools, a rope, and what looked like an old, metal army ammunition box.

"Sit down," he ordered. The flashlight cast angular shadows across Uncle Carl's face. He turned the light on Alex, but not for long enough to recognize him. The cap was pulled low over Alex's forehead, so that probably helped. He had also changed over the past three years. His hair was longer, he'd grown taller and broader, and he even sounded different when he spoke.

Alex dropped to the floor, and just like that, he was back in the past – when he had first found out that his uncle and father had robbed a Kenora bank and run off with the money. But Uncle Carl had changed over the past three years too. His hair was cut very short and he had gotten rid of his mustache. In the dim light, he looked like Alex's father.

Alex had a sudden urge to strike out at the man in front of him. Uncle Carl might be his dad's brother, but he had no right to look like him. Not after what he'd made Alex's father do. After his arrest, Uncle Carl had said the whole robbery was his brother's idea. But Alex was convinced that his uncle must have come up with the plot to rob the bank. Without Uncle Carl, Alex's father would never have chosen to abandon his family.

Uncle Carl tied Alex's ankles with a quick twist and ran the rope up the back of his legs. He pulled his wrists behind his back to tie them too. "That'll hold you," he muttered, "while I figure out what to do with you."

Leaving Alex in the corner, his uncle rolled up the sleeping bag and piled the tools and boxes near the door. He kept muttering under his breath. Alex only caught some words – something about a nosy kid.

Suddenly, Alex froze. Over the clatter of his uncle's preparations, he could hear another noise, faint at first, but getting louder. "Hello! Where are you?"

His uncle froze and then cocked his head. He turned to Alex before barreling out of the cabin. "You lying little creep! I thought you said you were alone!"

"Run, Jerry!" Alex shouted, but it was too late.

Jerry screamed. A minute later, Uncle Carl shoved him through the doorway and Jerry stumbled in, dropping the boot he was clutching.

"So your friend hurt his foot and went back to the camp, did he?" Uncle Carl snarled at Alex as he rummaged for more rope.

"I *thought* he went back," Alex replied, trying to keep his voice from shaking.

"Let me go!" Jerry cried. His eyes shone with terror. Maybe he would calm down if Alex kept his cool.

"Give him a break," Alex said. "Can't you see he's hurt?"

"I see that, all right. I don't think he'll get far anyway." He finished tying Jerry up and pulled him across the floor, away from Alex. "You two stay where you are. I'll be back." He dragged a wooden crate and a metal army box to the cabin doorway and disappeared from the cabin.

"What happened?" Jerry whispered frantically, his voice tight and his face twisted with pain. "Why has he tied us up?"

"I don't know." Alex paused. He didn't know if he should tell Jerry who the man was. Yes, he was his uncle – but not the same uncle Alex had grown up with. Uncle Carl was the one who had shown him how to dribble a basketball. He was the one who took Alex to the circus when his father couldn't get off work.

But that wasn't the man Uncle Carl was now. Alex could only guess what three years in prison had done to him. The angry voice and the rough manner in which he'd tied the boys up didn't make him seem like the uncle Alex once knew.

No, he wouldn't tell Jerry anything right now. If Jerry found out, he'd only panic more.

"Whatever he's up to," Alex whispered, "he doesn't want us around. But I think he's scared to let us go. He said he just needs one more night."

"Those shovels and stuff. Is he the one doing

all the digging on the island?"

"I guess so."

"What's in the boxes?" Jerry's voice was calmer now.

"I think ..." Alex began, but stopped as his uncle appeared in the doorway. "Shh!" Alex hissed.

"One more trip and I'll be back for you two," his uncle said, staggering out with a pile of shovels and tools.

"You think what?" Jerry whispered.

Alex hesitated. What *was* his uncle doing on Loon Island? The cops hadn't found him anywhere near here three years ago. He'd been caught on a boat farther south, miles and miles away.

"I think ... maybe ... he must have some money in the boxes. Or else he's searching for money when he digs. But don't let on to him you know anything. About the lights or the holes or *anything*! Play dumb. The less he thinks we know, the better. Maybe he'll let us go if he thinks we really don't know anything."

Jerry grimaced and squirmed, searching for a position that would ease the pain in his ankle.

"Why'd you take your boot off?" Alex nodded in the direction of Jerry's foot. "Your ankle's going to swell and you won't get the boot on again."

Uncle Carl returned before Jerry could answer.

He loosened the rope around Jerry's ankle and led him, limping, out the door. He returned for Alex next. "Come on, kid," he snapped. "And no funny stuff!"

"My friend's boot," Alex said as his uncle pulled on his arm. He crouched down awkwardly to retrieve it. His wrists were still bound behind his back. It was all he could do to grab the boot and then hold on to it.

Alex kept his head low and turned away from his uncle. As they neared the water, he saw the faint outline of a small, faded green motorboat. It was tied near the shore side of the pier, so they didn't have to cross the hole-ridden dock. Once they settled in, the boat sat low in the water, weighed down with three passengers and a pile of boxes. His uncle threw a canvas over some of the gear, but Alex glimpsed the barrel of a rifle under it. He gulped but said nothing.

"Hope this tub can carry us all," his uncle growled as he fiddled with the motor. He glanced at the boys. "Any trouble from you two and I'll gag and blindfold you both. Though in this soup, you'll never see where we're going, anyway."

Alex sneaked several looks at Uncle Carl from under the peaked cap. He kept discovering changes he hadn't noticed before. New lines had formed across his face and touches of gray peppered his hair. On his cheek was a scar the size of a coin that hadn't been there before.

The motor started with a sputter and the boat pulled away from the pier, sluggishly at first, then gradually picking up speed. Loon Island was quickly swallowed up by the fog. The boat seemed to be trapped in a cloud.

Alex shivered. He hoped Uncle Carl knew what he was doing. Three years ago the police had only caught him because he got lost among the islands and ran out of gas. Wherever they were going, Alex hoped it would be warm and dry. The damp, early morning chill had begun to penetrate his windbreaker. The speed of the motorboat only made it worse.

The sadness and betrayal Alex had felt three years ago resurfaced. The past was repeating itself and he didn't know what he could do to stop it.

CHAPTER 7

A GIANT FACE appeared through the fog, looming above the boat like an ancient god. Jerry recoiled before he realized what it was – the spirit rock painting of Devil's Gap. At least now they had an idea where they were.

They'd been traveling perhaps twenty minutes and had passed several islands, but until the face appeared, Alex had had no idea which way they were headed. Now he tried to concentrate on the direction they came from and the direction in which they were going. This was difficult in the fog and he suspected that Uncle Carl was deliberately detouring around islands or rocks to confuse them.

After another twenty minutes or so, his uncle eased up on the throttle. He turned the boat into a tiny inlet on a fair-sized island. A large spruce tree tilted outwards from the rocky shore, cloaking a sagging pier. Uncle Carl edged the boat up to it. He snagged the boat around a post and climbed gingerly out onto the rotting planks.

"OK, you two," he ordered. "Out! One at a time!"

Alex struggled out, still clutching Jerry's boot awkwardly behind his back. Jerry followed, wincing whenever he put weight on his left foot. Even in the fog Alex could see that the ankle was swollen. Jerry wouldn't be able to walk far without hurting it more.

An old shed stood beside the pier, behind the leaning spruce tree. The wood was gray-brown and faded, but its doors and windows were still intact.

"Get inside," Uncle Carl ordered, unlocking what looked like a new padlock on the door. Inside, in the dim light, Alex spotted a box of groceries, a new-looking camp stove, a few tools, and a Coleman lantern. He could also see a couple of blankets and a jacket thrown over a rickety chair.

"Down on the floor!" his uncle barked. "Away from each other."

Alex's mind was still in turmoil. There must be something they could do. Maybe he could somehow get the rope off his ankles and make a run for it. But his hands were tied and Jerry would never be able to keep up, not with that ankle. He eased himself down against a wall, expecting his friend to do the same.

But Jerry, with sudden courage, remained standing. "Listen, Mister, you can't just lock us up! That's kidnapping! Besides, you're the one who was trespassing on Loon Island, not us!"

"Jerry!" Alex cautioned urgently. "Shut up!"

His uncle's laugh startled him. It wasn't a

pleasant laugh. "Kid," he said to Jerry, "your friend's right. Keep your mouth shut! Unless you want me to shut it for you." He shoved Jerry to the floor. Then he retightened the ankle rope on both boys and double-checked the knots on their wrists. Alex kept his head low, but he needn't have worried. Uncle Carl didn't seem to care who they were. Too much else on his mind, probably.

"I'll decide what to do with you later," he said. "Right now, I'm getting some shut-eye." He rolled out the sleeping bag and placed it on the floor directly in front of the shed door. Before long, he was snoring.

With no other choice, the boys stretched out too – as much as they could. But the floor was hard and the rope pinched. "Try to rest," Alex whispered. "We'll need energy later. We've gotta get away from here."

But it was hard to get comfortable, never mind sleep. And his mind was churning. How could they get themselves out of this mess?

* * *

Hours later a loud rumble sounded from Alex's stomach and almost at once an answering one from Jerry's. "We hear you, we hear you," muttered Jerry.

"But there's nothing we can do about it."

"Any idea what time it is?" Alex whispered. With his hands tied, he couldn't read his watch.

"Noon? One o'clock? I dunno. I've been sleeping for a while. Feels like forever."

The light streaming through the window, which Alex thought faced west, was brighter now than it had been when they fell asleep. He couldn't actually *see* out the window, but he guessed the fog had thinned.

Alex shifted uneasily. "This floor is murder. My butt is killing me. How's the ankle?"

"Sore. Swollen, I think. And I'm starved."

"Me too." Alex wished his uncle would wake up and give them some food. Still, a part of him wanted Uncle Carl to keep sleeping. As long as he slept, Alex and Jerry could at least whisper. Maybe they could figure out a plan.

His uncle had said he needed only one more night. That must mean he'd found what he wanted – and what he was looking for could only be the quarter million that he'd stolen from the Kenora bank.

But the two boys had definitely put a crimp in his plans. Alex didn't know if his uncle would let them go when he was ready to make his getaway. The uncle Alex used to know wouldn't harm innocent boys. Alex wouldn't put it past him now, though – if prison had changed what Carl looked like, no doubt it had changed the rest of him too.

Poor Mom, Alex thought. What was she going through? Or had she even realized he was missing? She would just think he was off on his own again. But the Wylies? They might start worrying sooner.

He wished he or Jerry had left a note to say where they were going. It might be the afternoon before anyone became concerned. And even if anyone did realize the boys were missing, how long would it take them to search the various islands? How long before they would call in the police? How much would the fog interfere with the search?

Alex wished he hadn't been so concerned about getting in trouble with Mrs. Barkley. He should have told her about the strange holes and the sleeping bag in the cabin. And he should have shown his mother the medallion. At least then they would have some idea what might've happened to the boys. *Get a grip*, he told himself. *Regrets won't help at this stage.*

"Is he gonna sleep all day?" Jerry whispered, breaking in on Alex's thoughts. "What's he up to, anyway?"

"He was probably up all night. Digging for

the money."

"You said that before too," Jerry said, forgetting to whisper. "What money are you talking about?"

"Ssshhh. I'll tell you later. It's too much to explain now." They both glanced over at Uncle Carl. Had he heard them? He still appeared to be sound asleep.

The boys settled back down to wait. Alex tried to ignore the dull ache in his stomach. After what felt like half an hour – though it could have been ten minutes for all Alex knew – his uncle roused. He crawled out of the sleeping bag and went directly to the box of groceries. Had he been listening after all?

"S'pose you boys are hungry." He took out a can opener and opened three cans of baked beans. "I'll loosen one hand for you to eat, but no funny business. Or that's the last time I'll feed you." He located three spoons and gave each boy a can.

Alex had never tried cold beans, but he couldn't be picky. Who knew when they might eat next? Aware that his uncle was watching, he kept his head lowered as he wolfed down the food.

"Could we have a drink?" Jerry asked.

"I guess so." Uncle Carl found a mug in his stash, filled it with water from a water jug, and passed it to Jerry.

"You too?" He handed the mug to Alex and waited while he drank.

"I need a toilet," Alex said.

His uncle studied them a moment. "Fine," he said finally. Alex guessed Uncle Carl had decided they weren't that dangerous. He untied their feet, retied their hands, and took them one at a time to a primitive outhouse in the trees behind the shed.

This is my chance, thought Alex. *With my feet free, maybe I can make a run for it. Though how I'd get my hands loose ... And how I'd free Jerry ...*

But Uncle Carl's grip on his shoulder remained tight all the way there and back. As soon as they were in the cabin, he retied both their hands and feet.

Afterwards, he put the spoons and mug away and tossed the empty cans by the door. Then he sat down on the old chair and looked hard at the boys. "And now," he said, "I've gotta figure out what to do with you two."

"Why not just let us go?" Jerry said. "We don't know anything."

Uncle Carl perked up. "Anything about what?" he snapped.

"Anything about anything," Jerry said, but he didn't sound too convincing.

"I'm not so sure about that. You two come snooping around and ..."

"It's the truth," Jerry protested, beginning to sound desperate. "Ask Alex – he'll say the same thing."

"Alex?" Uncle Carl paused. He shot to his feet so fast he knocked over the old chair he'd been sitting on. "No, it couldn't be ..." He stared hard at Alex, then strode across the floor and snatched the double-billed detective cap from his head. With a single motion he swept Alex's sandy hair away from his forehead, wrenched back his neck, and gaped at him.

Alex stared back. "Hello, Uncle Carl," he said. "When did you get out of prison?"

CHAPTER 8

UNCLE CARL STOOD with his mouth open, his face turning red. "What are *you* doing on Loon Island?" he demanded harshly.

"I could ask you the same thing!" Alex answered in an equally harsh voice. His uncle ignored the question.

"What were you really doing in that old cabin?" Uncle Carl asked.

"What's it to you?" Uncle Carl wrenched Alex's head back further. "We're on vacation – we were just exploring," Alex said.

"Does your mother know where you were?"

"Of course," Alex lied. "And she'll be looking for me now." *I hope so*, Alex thought.

"Who's this other kid?"

"He's from Winnipeg. His family's on vacation at Family Camp too."

"Great! Two kids on vacation with nothing to do but snoop around where they shouldn't be," his uncle growled, turning away for a moment to gaze out the window.

After a few minutes, he turned back abruptly and crouched beside Alex. "How's your mother?'

Alex blinked at the sudden change in tone. "She's OK," he said sullenly. "She hasn't been sick."

"That's not what I mean and you know it. How is she adjusting these past three years without ...? On her own, I mean?" He put his hand on Alex's shoulder, but Alex promptly shrugged it off.

"She's all right, I guess. What do you care?"

"I thought you would've moved somewhere else by now."

"You thought wrong," Alex snapped. "Not enough money."

There was a moment of silence. Alex, feeling bolder, continued. "What are *you* doing here, anyway? Did you break out of prison or something?"

"I'm out early – for good behavior. That's the way it works, kid."

"Lucky you!" Alex said sarcastically.

Uncle Carl gave him a strange look. "What about your dad's life insurance?" he asked.

"They didn't pay up," Alex muttered. Then he added, with anger his uncle couldn't miss, "Under the circumstances, you know!"

"I never thought of that ... Those insurance guys never lose, do they!" He spat out the words.

"I guess not," said Alex. He glared at Uncle Carl, who shifted his eyes away.

"That wasn't part of my plan," his uncle muttered.

Alex's heart stopped. "What? What do you mean part of *your* plan?"

Uncle Carl rose abruptly. "I don't mean nothing. Shut up, kid. And your friend too." He grabbed a couple of tools and stormed out of the shed.

"Wait!" Alex shouted. But it was useless. The padlock on the door clicked shut and the roar of the boat's motor soon followed. The sound faded away into the distance.

"What's going on?" Jerry demanded. Alex started – he had forgotten Jerry was there with him. His mind was still swirling, trying to figure out what his uncle had meant by "*my* plan." "Why didn't you tell me he was your uncle?"

"I ... I don't know," Alex answered lamely. "I ..."

"What else have you been hiding?" Jerry sounded disgusted.

Alex didn't say anything.

"I thought we were friends. Friends don't keep dirty secrets from each other."

Alex sighed. "I was going to tell you. I just didn't know when." He stopped and realized he was telling the truth. He *was* going to tell Jerry, eventually. He just hadn't expected to be telling him this way, tied up in a shed after being kidnapped.

He took a moment before he began. "Three years ago, before I turned eleven, there was an armed robbery at a bank in Kenora. It was payday at the paper mill, so the bank had brought in extra cash. A masked thief held it up just after the Brink's truck delivered the money. He escaped with nearly a quarter of a million dollars."

Jerry didn't say anything, but he looked stunned. Alex continued.

"Well, he had a boat stashed close by and used it to get away. The police found the getaway car near the lakeshore." Alex closed his eyes for a moment, then continued slowly, almost as if he were talking to himself. "The police set off in their boat to chase the thief. It was raining hard, so they found it difficult to follow him. Two nights passed before they caught up to him, a lot farther south from here. Then they were surprised because they found *two* boats and *two* men – my dad and Uncle Carl." Alex stopped, looking at the floor.

"Then what?" Jerry said after a long pause.

"The boats had both stopped. One boat was empty and both men were in the other one. They were arguing about something and didn't see the cops at first. When they heard the police boat coming, they tried to escape. Only somehow, the boats collided and one of the men fell into the lake."

Alex's voice trailed off.

"So did the cops get 'em both?" Jerry asked softly.

"The one who fell in was my dad. I guess he hit his head or something, 'cause he was a good swimmer but he still drowned. He was dead by the time they found him." Alex blinked rapidly. "Uncle Carl was the second man. When the police caught him he said it was Dad who robbed the bank and he was just helping him escape. He said they were trying to get to Minnesota, only they'd gotten lost among all the islands and run out of gas."

"And the money?"

"They never found it. Uncle Carl said that Dad double-crossed him and planned to escape with all the money for himself. That he'd hid it somewhere the first night without telling Uncle Carl where. He said that's what they were arguing about when they were caught."

"And people believed him?"

"Well ... my mom and I didn't. It didn't sound like my dad at all. But then, it didn't sound like Uncle Carl either. And nobody could prove any different. Uncle Carl pleaded guilty to helping in the getaway. He got five years. Well, it was *supposed* to be five years ..."

"And now your uncle's back looking for the

money," Jerry finished.

"Yeah. He either figured out where my dad hid it or he knew all along."

"Maybe your uncle was lying."

"Maybe. Who knows? It doesn't really matter who robbed the bank and who helped with the escape. Any way you look at it, my dad was involved. He deserted us. Maybe Uncle Carl talked him into it, maybe he didn't ... Mom says Uncle Carl was a smooth talker." Alex's voice broke. He paused. For a while, neither one of them said anything. Alex waited, tensely, for Jerry's response.

"What do you think he'll do with us?" Jerry asked finally.

Alex shrugged and tried to look more confident than he felt. "I dunno. I don't *think* he'll hurt us, but ..."

"Wait – did you know all this time it was him on the island?" Jerry interrupted. "When we found the holes?"

"Not the first time. I got suspicious when I found the medallion. The medallion was Uncle Carl's. My dad had one just like it. My grandpa gave one to each of them before he died. It has kind of a made-up family crest on the front."

"Why didn't you tell me sooner?" Jerry asked, frustration creeping into his voice again. "Why didn't you tell me about your dad and everything?"

"People think of you differently when you tell them your dad's a crook. They look at you differently, talk to you differently. Some people you thought were friends stop coming around at all."

Jerry stayed quiet again. But when Alex looked at him, he could see the frustration hadn't left Jerry's face. He'd expected that, expected to be pushed away, but he still felt disappointed.

Alex closed his eyes. The shed darkened as more and more time passed.

"The fog must be getting thick again," Alex muttered, breaking the silence. He sat up straighter and tried to stretch out his cramped legs. It was hard, though, with his hands and feet tied.

Jerry squirmed around too. Without looking at Alex, he said, "It doesn't change anything, you know. Even if your dad did it, it wasn't your fault. But you should have told me."

Alex opened his mouth to answer but he didn't know what to say.

"You hear something?" Jerry asked abruptly.

Alex listened. The muffled roar of a motor slowly grew louder.

"Could it be the police? Or somebody searching for us?" Jerry's voice was suddenly hopeful.

"It's probably Uncle Carl. He left all his stuff

behind, so he must be coming back."

The motor shut off and Alex heard a thump on the pier as someone climbed out. They heard nothing but silence. Any hope Alex had felt trickled away. If someone was looking for them, they would have been calling out their names. The padlock clicked open and Alex's uncle strode in.

CHAPTER 9

THE SCENT OF frying sausages seeped into the shed. Alex's stomach gurgled.

"You smell that?" Jerry muttered. "Is he trying to torture us, or what?"

"Let's hope he plans to share," Alex said.

His uncle, wherever he'd been, had returned in a good mood. He was whistling an unfamiliar tune, and when Jerry asked if they could stretch their legs, he'd surprised Alex by untying their ankles. He still checked to make sure their hands were secure behind their backs, though. Now he had locked them inside the shed and gone outside with the camp stove and grocery box.

The boys limped around inside, trying to get rid of the stiffness in their legs. Their backs ached after hours of sitting on a hard floor.

"What time do you think it is?" Alex asked. With his hands tied, he couldn't see his watch.

"Evening, sometime," suggested Jerry.

"We've got to get out of here," Alex whispered. "We could steal his boat and take off."

"Can you run a boat?"

Alex shook his head. "I used to watch my dad,

but that was a long time ago. We'll have to use the oars."

"I don't think I can move very fast with this ankle," Jerry said. "If you get a chance to go without me, then go for help."

"I can't leave you," Alex said, surprised.

"You'll have to or we'll never be found. You can bring a rescue team back for me."

Alex hesitated. "I guess ..."

"It's the only way."

"Fine," Alex said. "But it works the other way too. If you have a chance to get away, then *you* go for help."

His uncle unlocked the door and carried in two bowls heaped with sausages and canned spaghetti. "Sit against the wall," he ordered after freeing their hands. Surprisingly, he didn't retie their ankles. "You try anything, you're both dead meat," he added.

The boys grabbed their bowls and stuffed the food down. Uncle Carl watched for a couple of minutes, then went back outside.

"Now's our chance," whispered Alex. He took one last swallow and set down his bowl. Then, he grabbed Jerry's hiking boot and scuttled behind the door. Jerry followed, still limping.

They were just in time. The padlock screeched

and the door creaked open. Uncle Carl, carrying a nearly empty saucepan, took one step inside. "What the ..." he exclaimed, ducking sideways just as Alex brought the boot down. Alex had aimed for his uncle's head, but the boot grazed his ear, striking him on the shoulder instead. The boot and the saucepan both went flying across the shed.

The force knocked Uncle Carl forward and Alex leaped at his back, trying to push him onto the floor. Jerry grabbed the man's leg and twisted. Uncle Carl swore loudly, kicking sideways as he went down. His leg struck Jerry's already injured ankle and Jerry grunted with pain. He let go and rolled to his side, grimacing. Alex could tell at a glance that Jerry wouldn't be able to run for it.

Alex hesitated. He knew he should go for the boat, but that would mean leaving Jerry behind.

"Go!" Jerry shouted. He raised himself with a struggle and threw his weight on Alex's uncle.

I'm on my own, Alex thought. *It's now or never.* He turned to make a dash for it, but his foot caught on the threshold and he fell forward. As soon as he had clambered to his feet, he raced for the pier.

The boat was tied to a leaning post. A quick glance revealed that the oars were in the bottom. He made a grab for the rope as he braked to a stop.

He hoped that the knot was the kind that released easily, but it held. He could hear his uncle yelling at Jerry, who must have tackled Uncle Carl again.

Alex struggled with the knots but the rope was wet. His fingers slipped on the knots. If only he had a knife ...

He shot a glance back. His uncle was dragging himself through the shed door with Jerry clinging to his leg.

With one last effort, Alex managed to loosen the knot. He pulled the rope free and made a flying leap into the boat just as Uncle Carl shook Jerry off. Alex landed heavily in the bow and hot pain spread along his ribs. The boat shook from side to side as he scrambled to sit up. He snatched an oar and tried to use it to shove the boat away from the pier.

But he was too slow. His uncle dashed down the rickety pier, jumped into the hip-deep water, and grabbed the edge of the boat. The boat swung wildly around and Alex tumbled to the bottom, landing on his side. Before he could scramble to his knees, Uncle Carl grabbed him in a vice-like grip.

"Get out, Alex," he ordered harshly. "Back to the shed. And no more tricks."

* * *

Uncle Carl dragged the two boys back to the old shed. This time, he tied the rope around their wrists and ankles so tightly it bit into their skin. He gave them a warning glare before leaving the shed.

Alex glanced at Jerry. He wanted to apologize for messing up. But Jerry was looking at his ankle, which had now turned an ugly blue-green. Alex sighed and closed his eyes. The only thing they could do was rest and hope for another chance to escape.

Some time later the door opened again. Uncle Carl came in and sorted through the pile of tools on the floor. Then he picked up a hammer and some nails and went back out. Alex pretended to be asleep. Jerry, too, was quiet.

Before long Alex heard a pounding coming from the front wall of the shed. "What's he up to?" he asked, shifting uncomfortably. His ribs hurt from when he'd landed on them in the boat. He struggled to sit up, and when he did, he saw that Uncle Carl was boarding up the window.

Jerry sat up too. "Is he going to leave us locked in here?"

"Looks like it." Alex hesitated, then added, "Unless he decides to get rid of us more ... permanently."

Jerry shook his head. "I don't think he means

to hurt us."

Alex looked sharply at his friend. "Why do you think that?"

"Because … if he wanted to hurt us, he would have done it already. He even fed us. And, yeah, he was angry when we tried to escape, but all he did was tie us back up again."

Alex breathed deeply. "Don't underestimate him. He's not who he used to be."

"I just mean … he's your uncle. Maybe you could try reasoning with him."

Alex snorted. "That would work, if he was reasonable."

The pounding at the window stopped, but then began again at the far corner of the shed. It sounded as if Uncle Carl was securing the whole place. With the window boarded up and dusk approaching, it was now quite dark inside.

After some time, Uncle Carl unlocked the door and carried in the grocery box. He lit the lantern and began to sort through the contents of the box. He placed a loaf of bread, a box of cookies, and some chocolate bars on the chair. The cans, along with the bowls and spoons, he returned to the box.

"Those are for you," he said, indicating the groceries on the chair. "If nobody finds you for a while, you've got enough for a couple of days."

"You can't just leave us here. We could die!" Jerry protested.

"Be quiet!" Uncle Carl shot back. "I'm going to untie you two and I'm leaving you food. In a day or two I'll notify somebody where you are. They'll find you – this island isn't that isolated. There are a couple of blankets there and I'll leave this water container."

"Are you going now?" Jerry asked, sounding panicked.

"Soon as I'm ready and soon as it's dark."

Alex broke his stony silence. "Can you take us to the outhouse again first?" he asked. His mind was working furiously. He was still searching for a way to escape, but he also wanted to stop Uncle Carl from getting away. Alex needed answers from him, and if he got away, there would be no answers.

"One at a time, like before," his uncle responded. "You first, then your friend. After this, you'll have to use the corner." He untied Alex's feet and hands, but this time he leashed a rope around Alex's neck.

"Tell me what really happened three years ago, Uncle Carl," Alex said on the way to the outhouse. "Why did you rob that bank?"

"Kid," his uncle said, his voice more tired than angry, "you heard what I said at the trial. I'm not saying anything more."

"But I'm asking for the truth. My mom and I –"

Uncle Carl jerked the rope. Alex knew that meant it was time to stop asking. He had to think of a plan, and it had to be soon.

When he got to the shed, he told Jerry to stall. "Take your time," he whispered. "Be slow. Cough or talk on your way back, so I can hear you coming."

Once the two had left, Alex looked around the shed. His uncle had left the lantern on and it cast dark shadows on the floor and walls. As soon as the padlock clicked, Alex started fumbling through the tools. When he found what he was looking for, he slipped it into his jacket pocket. Alex just had to hope his uncle wouldn't look through the pile again and notice anything missing.

Next he removed the caps from the water container and from the red gasoline container sitting by the door. His hands shook as he poured water into the gasoline. Uncle Carl hadn't left them with that much water. But this was the best plan he could think of.

A small puddle formed around the gas container. If only he had a funnel to pour the water ...

He heard Jerry cough. His hand shook again and water splashed onto the floor. Quickly, he screwed on the gasoline cap and wiped the floor with his jacket sleeve.

When the door opened, he was pouring him-self a drink of water. His uncle glanced at him suspiciously. "What are you doing?" he asked.

"I was thirsty." Alex tried to sound casual. "Is it OK if I have a drink of water?"

CHAPTER 10

UNCLE CARL LEFT as soon as he had loaded his equipment and supplies into the boat. He didn't check through the boxes before carrying them out and didn't notice that the gasoline can was a little heavier than before. It was too dark for him to see the mark on the floor where Alex had spilled water.

"Don't pig out on the food," his uncle warned. "Or the water, either. Make it last." Alex scoffed. His uncle almost sounded worried.

The shed door shut behind him, leaving the boys in total darkness. And then the lock clicked shut. A few minutes later, the boat's motor started and soon the noise faded into the distance.

"We might as well try to sleep," muttered Jerry. "We can't do much till morning, anyway. Even if we got out, it would be too dark to escape."

"Where's that chair with the blankets?" asked Alex. "We should have gotten them before he left with the light."

"Just hold on a minute."

Alex heard Jerry fumbling around in the dark, near the chair. Suddenly a narrow beam of light flooded the shed. "Where'd you get that?"

Alex asked.

Jerry chuckled. "I snitched it from one of his boxes while you were at the outhouse."

"You think he'll come back for it?"

"He'll just think he dropped it somewhere in the dark. Besides, he had two flashlights. The second one is still in the box."

"Maybe you're right," Alex said. Then he snorted. "I wonder if he'll miss this." He zipped open his jacket pocket and held out the screwdriver he'd swiped.

"You too?" Jerry snickered. "So what are you ragging on me for?"

Alex grinned. "There's something else. I put water in his gasoline. If he adds more gas to the tank on his boat, that should stop him. I just don't know if I used enough water."

The boys continued to discuss ways to escape. But they'd have to wait until morning. What they needed most now was some sleep.

They slept restlessly. The night dragged as they tossed and turned on the hard floor. Neither boy dozed off until after midnight.

When Alex woke, the luminous dial on his watch read seven-fifteen. With the window boarded, it was still dark in the shed, but cracks of light were visible around the door. Alex sat up and felt around for the flashlight Jerry had stolen. He switched it on and examined the shed door.

"What're you doing?" Jerry mumbled, not fully awake.

"Trying to figure out how to get this door off its hinges. Here, I need you to hold the flashlight."

Jerry rose and came to stand beside Alex. "Do you know how to do that?"

"Not really. I'm hoping this screwdriver will help."

"Let me try. I saw my dad do it once."

While Alex held the light, Jerry struggled with the hinges and the screwdriver. "What we really need," he said, "is a hammer."

"What we *have*," Alex said, "is your hiking boot. Let's try that."

Jerry held the screwdriver against the bottom of the upper hinge bolt and pounded it with the boot. The screwdriver slipped several times. Finally it held and the bolt slid up.

"Got it!" he exclaimed. He switched to the bottom hinge, but it was more difficult. To reach it, Jerry had to lie on the floor, but the boot was big, so it was almost impossible to use it as a hammer now. After about ten minutes he stopped, breathing heavily.

"Let me try," said Alex.

"Let's eat something first. What'll it be? Cookies, bread, or chocolate bars? Take your choice."

Alex looked longingly at the chocolate bars. "We'd better start with the bread, I guess. It'll spoil first. Bread and water – a meal fit for a prisoner!" Feeling discouraged, he sat back and chewed on the dry bread. It was starting to look like there might be no escape after all.

"Turn the flashlight off," Jerry said. "If we don't get out of here, we'll want it tonight."

Alex switched it off. He leaned back and tried to come up with a plan. The thought of another night in this place didn't comfort him.

"The chair!" Jerry yelled all of a sudden. "Let's try the chair!"

"What?"

"The chair. We can use it to try breaking through the window. Your uncle had new nails, but he used old boards that he found outside, right? The chair might smash through if the wood is rotten enough."

Alex sat up straight. "That could work."

"I'll shine the light," Jerry suggested. "You try the chair. But watch out – the glass will break first."

Alex swung the chair back and launched it at the window. Just as he'd predicted, the glass shattered to the floor. The boards on the outside didn't move.

"You'd better let me move the glass," Alex said, glancing at Jerry's feet. He was still wearing only one boot. "You might cut your foot."

Using the boot, he knocked out the remaining pieces of glass and then used his jacket to sweep them into a pile by the wall. Then he picked up the chair by the legs. "Here goes!" He smashed the chair several times against the boards.

"It's working!" Jerry shouted. The boards began to splinter but so did the chair. After a couple more blows, the back fell off and then the chair legs split. Alex pounded several more times and the chair broke into bits.

Two boards gaped open – not nearly enough – but gray light flooded into the room.

"Pass me your boot again," Alex grinned at Jerry. "That was a brilliant idea to use the chair."

He hammered away at the boards with the boot. Then he used the screwdriver to pry some of them apart. Finally, using his jacket to protect his hands, he pulled off a couple more boards. At last the hole looked large enough to squeeze through.

"Let's get out of here." Alex started to poke his head through the gap.

"Just wait." Jerry pulled him back. "You're forgetting something. If we don't find a way off this island, I'd sooner sleep in here than out in the bush. Can we get back in, if we want to?"

"If we can get out, we can get back in. We'll stand on a log or something if we have to."

"OK," Jerry said, "but we'd better take the food with us to be safe."

"You're right. It's a good thing somebody's brain is switched on this morning." He paused. "How's the ankle?"

"Not as sore as last night. But I don't think I can put my boot on yet." Jerry sat down to try but the leather was too stiff. He winced as he struggled with the boot.

"Try my sneakers," Alex said. "They might be easier on your ankle – if they fit."

Alex pulled on the hiking boots while Jerry tried the sneakers. Alex had wanted to try the boots since he first saw them – but not under these circumstances. They were stiff, like Jerry said, but they were sturdy and they fit.

The sneakers fit Jerry too. "That feels better," he said, moving his foot around gingerly.

"With that ankle, you'd better go first," Alex said. He gave Jerry a boost and helped him wriggle through the window. Jerry dropped heavily to the ground but stood up right away.

"I'm OK," he said.

Alex handed him the water, food, and flashlight, and then squeezed through the hole. "My ribs hurt," he said as he emerged from the cabin. A big purple bruise had formed on his side.

Leaving the supplies in a pile beside the shed, the boys scrambled past the leaning spruce tree to the old pier. The lake was a still, dull gray in the morning light. The fog had lifted, but low, heavy clouds threatened rain and the air felt damp. The smell of wet spruce needles was everywhere. No birds sang.

"Talk about quiet," said Jerry. "Do you have any idea where we are?"

"No. But we came through the Devil's Gap about twenty minutes before we got here. I couldn't tell which direction we went but I don't think we're *too* far from the camp."

"They won't have any idea where to look for us, will they? They'd never expect us to leave Loon Island."

"Maybe they'll think we drowned," said Alex gloomily. "If only we had some way to let them know we're here."

Jerry searched through his jacket pocket and extracted the whistle his father had given him earlier in the week. "I forgot I had this," he said, grinning.

For the next five minutes he blew the whistle,

three sharp blasts at a time about every half minute. Feeling disheartened, he shoved the whistle back into his pocket. "All this is doing is giving me a headache," he groaned. "We need earplugs."

"I guess the best thing to do is explore this island," said Alex. "We can see if there's a way to get off, anyway."

"OK," Jerry agreed. "Which way will we go? I don't see any trails."

"We'd cover more ground if we each went in a different direction."

"But how will we find each other again?"

"Let's set a time limit," said Alex. "You walk that way for about fifteen minutes. I'll go this way. And stay as close to shore as you can. If we don't meet somewhere in that time, then it's too big an island for us to explore. Blow your whistle and I'll yell. If we don't hear each other, then we should turn around and meet back here."

Jerry turned to begin, but Alex stopped him. "One more thing. If you happen to see someone in a boat and you want to signal him …"

"Yeah?"

"Make sure it's not my uncle. He might still be around. And if you're not sure that it's him – hide in the bush."

CHAPTER 11

FIFTEEN MINUTES HAD just about passed when Alex caught sight of Jerry working his way toward him. The island was not actually very large, but with no trails, it was difficult to move fast. In one place a small sandbar edged the water and made walking easier, but for most of the way, rocks and leaning trees slowed Alex's progress.

"I didn't find a thing to help us," he said when the two boys met. "How about you?"

Jerry looked curiously at Alex. "How well can you swim – I mean, really swim?"

Alex shrugged. "Pretty well. Why?"

"Back there I can see another island. But there's at least three or four hundred yards of water in between. Maybe more."

"You think I should *swim* to it?"

"I saw a cabin there, maybe a quarter of a mile along. I couldn't see but there might be a boat-house and a pier too."

"Did you try blowing your whistle?" Alex asked.

"Yeah, but it didn't do any good. There's only one way to find out what's there." Jerry made overhand swimming motions with his arms.

"Let's go look," said Alex. He scrambled along behind Jerry, wondering how deep the water would be. He had never tried swimming that far before. Since his father's death, he avoided all bodies of water except for pools. And if his mother were here, she would have a fit. But if his mother were here, they wouldn't be in the trouble they were in. All he could do was try. It was better than doing nothing.

Alex couldn't gauge the depth of the water between the two islands. The shore was rocky on both sides, which suggested that the water was deep. Alex waited while Jerry tried blowing his whistle again. The lake looked calm, with no worrisome currents.

Alex peeled down to his undershorts. He left his clothes and watch as well as Jerry's boots in a pile. "Be careful," Jerry cautioned as Alex waded in. "My mom says more people drown close to shore than in the middle of a lake."

"I didn't really need to know that," Alex said, grimacing.

In a lake this big, the water never warmed up much, even on hot days. But he ignored the cold as he entered the water and started swimming, using the front crawl. His bruised ribs ached but he tried to ignore that. By the time Alex was barely halfway across, his breath had shortened and his arms felt heavy. He panted as he turned onto his back to rest, the way he'd learned in swimming lessons. *Maybe I should just float to the other side*, he thought to himself.

"Alex!" Jerry's voice roused him. "Are you going to take all day?"

"I'm going," he called back. He flipped back onto his stomach and started the crawl again. Slowly the other island grew closer. He hauled himself out of the water and onto a rock.

He waved to Jerry to signal that he was fine and started along the shore to where they had caught sight of a cabin. The damp air made him shiver and rocks bit into his bare feet.

As he neared the cabin, he was surprised to see that it looked brand-new – and as he moved closer, he realized it wasn't even finished. The windows were still mere holes and the boathouse was just a shell. "Hello!" he called twice and then stopped to listen for an answer. He found the pier easily, but there was no boat. The place was deserted.

Alex waited by the pier for a few minutes, catching his breath. He might as well start back. He took a few steps, but then turned around once more. *One look inside the cabin won't take long*, he thought. *At least I might find a clue where we are.*

The door opened easily. Whoever was building the cabin hadn't bothered to lock up.

Alex stood in the doorway and looked around. The inside was just one large, open area, not yet divided into rooms. The smell of new lumber was strong. A wooden table and an old chair stood in the center, but there were no maps or papers that might reveal the name of the island he was on.

Sighing, he headed outside, taking care to close the door behind him. He glanced around one last time. He had just turned to start back when he saw it – a glimpse of red in the shrubs on the far side of the cabin. He ran toward it, and just as he suspected, it was a faded red canoe, upside down and almost hidden.

He moved to examine it. It seemed to be in good shape and the paddles beside it looked new. Somebody had painted "The Dragon" on the side in large letters.

Alex felt hesitant about taking it – this was different than stealing the screwdriver from his uncle – but he and Jerry *needed* this canoe. He shivered. He couldn't stand around in his underwear trying to make up his mind. Unless he kept moving, he'd be chilled right through and unable to swim back.

He grabbed the prow and began to drag the

canoe out of the bushes. With a heave, he managed to turn it over. After that, it wasn't too difficult to move because the ground was wet and slippery and there was a slight downhill slant toward the water.

Leaving the canoe by the pier, he returned for the paddles. He wished he could leave a note to tell the owner – whoever he was – that he'd return "The Dragon."

Alex launched the canoe and climbed in carefully. He hadn't paddled a canoe *alone* before, but he'd watched his gym teacher do it. He knew paddling alone was different from paddling with someone. He knelt in the back, but farther forward than usual. He remembered his teacher saying that this was the best way to balance a canoe. He turned back along the shore toward Jerry.

At first the canoe zigzagged unevenly. He switched the paddle from side to side, but it wasn't easy. Water dripped onto the floor in front of him as he switched the paddle across. He recalled that a person alone was supposed to use a J-stroke, whatever that was. At least there was no wind to blow the canoe off course. By the time he got back to Jerry he was no longer chilled, but sweating.

"Where did you find *that*?" Jerry exclaimed. He jumped from side to side in a little victory dance while Alex beached the canoe. As Alex climbed out, Jerry burst out laughing.

"What's so funny?" Alex asked.

"You, paddling a canoe in your underwear. I wish I had my camera!"

"Just as well you don't," snorted Alex, putting his clothes and watch back on. "I didn't find any map. I'm still not sure where we are."

"We came through the Devil's Gap ..."

"Yeah, so that puts us east of Loon Island. Then after we passed through it, I *think* we came south. So we should try paddling north and west."

"Do you know which way that is?"

"Not for sure," Alex said. "It would be easier if the sun was out. But what do we have to lose? We're already lost."

"True," Jerry said with a grin. "I'll be happy to get off this island. Let's go back to the shed and get the food and flashlight.

"Yeah, and the blankets too. But we left them inside the shed."

"I can boost you in to get them. We'll need them if we have to stop anywhere on the way."

Or worse – spend the night out in the canoe, Alex thought as they headed toward the old shed.

CHAPTER 12

"HOW FAR DO you think we've come?" Jerry asked. It was six o'clock and the boys had paused to choke down another slice of dry bread.

Alex shrugged. "I can't tell in this fog. We passed several islands, but we probably didn't even see all of them. And who knows how large they were? Or if we're even headed the right way?"

Soon after the boys started canoeing, the clouds dropped, forming a thick fog. Occasionally the fog lifted, letting them see farther ahead. But then it settled down again, blanketing everything in a cloak of gray.

They'd spent the afternoon easing the canoe from island to island, never sure if they were headed in the right direction. One wide stretch had no islands and Alex feared they might be headed the wrong way altogether. They both felt a little nervous without life jackets, but they became more confident as their paddling improved, in part because the lake stayed calm. *Just so long as a storm doesn' t blow up*, Alex thought.

"Another couple of hours and it'll be dark," said Jerry. "What'll we do then?"

"We'll have to find somewhere to beach this canoe. We don't want to get caught on the water in the dark." Alex stopped for a moment to swallow a mouthful of bread. "Then we can turn the canoe over and sleep under it. Good thing we went back for the blankets. Even in July it gets chilly at night, 'specially when it's damp."

They resumed paddling, moving from island to island. Suddenly Jerry held up his paddle and signaled Alex to stop. "Listen!"

Somewhere in the distance a motor hummed. It was the first sign of human life all day. The fog had apparently kept tourists and fishermen close to shore or off the lake altogether.

"Blow your whistle," Alex urged.

"But what if it's your uncle? Earlier you said ..."

"That was hours ago. I don't think it's him. He must be miles away by now."

Jerry blew the whistle on and off for several minutes while Alex shouted "Hello! Hello!" over and over. But the noise had no effect. The hum of the motor faded away.

Feeling even more discouraged and tired than before, the boys began to paddle again. For all they could see, maybe they were going in circles.

It was after eight before Alex caught sight of an island with a shallow inlet that had enough of a sandbar to pull onto. They had just crossed a large stretch of open water and Alex was starting to worry that they might not see another island for a while.

"Let's pull the canoe out there," he suggested when he saw the sandbar. He wished he knew where they were. Twice they'd halted briefly at other small islands to check directions by the moss on the trees. But most of the trees had moss all around them.

"OK." Jerry spread his fingers painfully. His hands were covered with blisters. He hunched his shoulders and tried to massage his right arm.

Alex steered the canoe carefully past a couple of large rocks and up onto the sand. Both boys climbed out and pulled the canoe onto higher ground. "How much food do we have left?" Alex asked, slumping onto a rock.

"A couple of chocolate bars and the rest of the bread. We'd better save it."

Alex stood up abruptly. "I'm going to explore inland. Give me ten minutes and then blow your whistle. And lend me your cap."

"What for?" Jerry looked at him doubtfully.

"You'll see – I hope." Alex took the cap from Jerry's outstretched arm.

Alex didn't have to go far to find what he was looking for. "Come here," he called back to Jerry. "If your ankle can handle it."

He began picking the blueberries he had found. They weren't quite as ripe as he'd have liked, but they'd make a welcome addition to the dry bread. In fifteen minutes the boys had filled Jerry's cap and stuffed numerous handfuls into their mouths.

"Dee-licious!" Jerry exclaimed as they returned to the canoe. "Now, where's the ice cream?"

"Too bad we don't have any matches, either," Alex said. "A fire would be nice."

"Did you ever learn how to make one by rubbing sticks together?" Jerry asked hopefully.

"No. And even if we knew how, the wood's too wet."

They sat in silence for some time as the evening grew darker. Somewhere an owl hooted over and over, and once a loon gave its laughing cry. Then the mosquitoes began their relentless attack. It had been a long, discouraging day and the night didn't look promising either.

We haven't gotten anywhere, Alex thought. *We're still lost. Uncle Carl has probably got the money and escaped by now. And I never got him to tell me what really happened.* He sighed deeply and closed his eyes. It seemed that all their efforts – breaking out of the shed, swimming to the other island, finding the canoe, and paddling this far – were for nothing.

"Listen!" Jerry hissed suddenly. Once again Alex heard the distant hum of a motor. This time it was moving closer.

"Your whistle!" Alex exclaimed. Jerry began to blow in sharp blasts of three. The noise of the motor grew louder and Alex was afraid the sound would drown out the whistles. It was almost dark and he couldn't see either a boat or a light in the water. He shouted for help between each whistle blast. Then, abruptly, the motor shut off.

"Hello!" Alex yelled. "Help! Hello!"

"Hang on! I'm coming!" someone answered. The voice sounding eerie and disembodied in the fog. The motor began to purr again and a faint light pierced the dark. Alex could just make out a single person in the back of a small, dark-colored boat.

"Is that your uncle?" Jerry asked.

"Get ready to run for it," Alex said. "He'd never find us in the dark." He strained his eyes to see who was at the motor.

CHAPTER 13

THE DARK BOAT emerged slowly out of the fog. The boys were prepared to hide, if they needed to, but the lone occupant of the boat wore the uniform of an Ontario Provincial Police officer.

"We're saved!" Jerry shouted. He and Alex scrambled over to help land the boat.

The officer – a tall dark-haired man – introduced himself as Corporal Raynard. "What're you doing out here?" he asked, peering from boy to boy.

The officer listened without interrupting while Jerry explained what had happened. He ran his fingers over his short, black mustache as Jerry spoke, glancing every now and then at Alex.

"Don't you believe us?" Alex asked when Jerry stopped talking. The officer was looking at them suspiciously.

"It sounds pretty far-fetched," he said. "You boys aren't playing some trick on your parents that backfired in the fog, are you?"

"No!" Jerry protested. "Just ask our parents. They know we wouldn't do that."

"It's your parents that have me out here looking for you. They called ..."

"Where do you think we got this canoe?" interrupted Alex. "It isn't from Loon Island. They all have 'Family Camp' painted on the side."

"Good point." Corporal Raynard pulled on his mustache again. "For now, let's load your stuff into the boat and I'll take you back to the camp. You've got your parents worried sick." He paused. "If you *were* trying to get back to Loon Island, you were headed in the wrong direction."

"What'll we do with the canoe?"

"Someone can come back for it tomorrow. Just turn it over for now. It'll slow us down if we try to pull it. It's slow going already, in this fog."

The fog began to thin less than an hour later, as they neared Loon Island. The boat's light cut a longer, wider path ahead of them and flickered over the old buildings at the south end of the island. Alex grabbed Jerry's arm and pointed, but it was too difficult to discuss anything over the noise of the motor.

As they started up the east side of the island, a cool north wind cut through the boys' clothes and made Alex shiver. Corporal Raynard eased up on the motor and shouted over the noise. "Which side of the island had those supposed holes?"

"This side," Alex shouted back. "But you have to walk in a ways to see them."

"Just show me the inlet then."

The boat continued northward. In a few minutes Alex pointed ahead. "There it is. We'll take you in and show you the holes if you want."

The boat's lights swung briefly over the inlet, then veered back. "The fog's thinning out but it's too dark. I'll check it in the morning," the corporal shouted back.

Suddenly Jerry grabbed Alex. "Look!" He pointed toward the inlet. Alex fixed his eyes in the direction Jerry was pointing, but saw nothing. "There's a boat in there," Jerry insisted, pulling on the corporal's arm.

Corporal Raynard frowned but turned the boat back into the inlet. At first Alex couldn't see anything unusual. Then the light from the boat shone on a small, dark green motorboat hugging the shore.

"That's his boat!" Jerry shouted, and Alex's heart began to beat in slow, almost painful thumps. That *was* Uncle Carl's boat, but Uncle Carl was nowhere to be seen.

As they pulled in beside it, Alex could see the grocery box and several tools still piled in the front. At the rear stood the red gasoline can. Near it, the motor was tipped up as if someone had been examining it. It looked very much as if the water Alex had mixed with the fuel had done its job.

"Huh. Maybe you two *are* telling the truth," Corporal Raynard muttered. He switched on his large flashlight and focused it on the shore, but the band of light revealed nothing except trees and one small rock. He edged the boat closer and clambered out.

"You two stay here," he ordered, looping the boat's rope over the rock. A moment later he disappeared into the trees.

Alex and Jerry waited impatiently for about five minutes. They could hear Corporal Raynard struggling through the bushes, first one way and then the next. A few times they saw the flashlight beaming through the trees. Finally, he reappeared. "It's too dark and too thick to find anything," he said. "It'll have to wait until daylight."

"We could take you to the holes now," urged Jerry. "We know how to get there." He sounded excited. Alex wished he could feel the same way. Instead, he felt unbelievably tired and sort of sick.

"In the morning," the corporal repeated firmly.

"What about the boat?" asked Jerry.

"We'll take it with us. Just in case the guy comes back for it." There was no doubt in Corporal Raynard's voice anymore. The boat and its supplies proved that the boys' story was true.

Alex sat quietly, his mind in turmoil. If the boat

had been usable, Uncle Carl would have left ages ago. He'd had a whole night and the entire day to do whatever he'd planned and then to escape. So where was he now?

Alex glanced back at the boat trailing behind them. The tools and groceries were still in it. Did that mean that Uncle Carl couldn't carry them? Or that he was close by? Only the ammunition box was gone. If Alex's instincts were right, the money would be in the box with Uncle Carl.

Alex moved the puzzle to the back of his mind. He had something else to deal with right now. His mother would be expecting him – completely unprepared for what he had to tell her about where he had been.

CHAPTER 14

THE WHOLE CAMP seemed to be waiting for the boys when they followed Corporal Raynard up the steps and along the trail to the main lodge. Alex's mother had circles under her eyes and the long hug she gave him told him how frightened she'd been. But she stayed dry-eyed, unlike Jerry's mother, who burst out crying as soon as the two boys appeared. Mr. Wylie hung back a little, then hugged Jerry and squeezed Alex's shoulder.

Mrs. Barkley surprised him with a rib-crushing hug that hurt his bruises. Lindsey and Beth jumped up and down, clung to his hand, and stuffed cookies and donuts into his mouth. He was embarrassed by all the attention.

He was embarrassed, too, when Corporal Raynard insisted that the boys tell their story again so that he could write down the details. The shadows under his mother's eyes only deepened the longer he spoke.

"Does he have a gun?" the corporal asked.

"I think I saw a rifle in the boat," Alex admitted.

"And he's got a hunting knife, for sure," broke in Jerry.

Finally, the corporal ran out of questions. "I'll want your help in the morning," he reminded the boys. "Right after breakfast. Mrs. Barkley's offered me a room, so I don't have to face the fog back to Kenora." Then he went into Mrs. Barkley's office to call in a report on the camp's two-way radio. Cell phones didn't work here, Alex guessed.

After that, everyone retired to the cabins. Alex had to tell the story again for Lindsey and Beth. He gave them a shorter version and left out some of the details he thought would scare them. Eventually the girls were too tired to hear more and they settled down to sleep.

Alex and his mother went outside and sat on the steps. The other cabins couldn't be seen in the dark. The fog seemed to be lifting, and once in a while, moonlight showed between the branches. An owl hooted softly in the distance.

A long time had passed since Alex felt this comfortable opening up to his mother. But something had changed over the past two days.

"It's weird," he told her. "I feel so mixed up. I have this feeling that Uncle Carl is hiding something about Dad. I tried asking him but ..."

There was a long pause. Finally, Alex continued. "When Uncle Carl left us locked in the cabin, I should have been furious at him. I *was*

123

furious. But a part of me felt sorry for him too. I don't understand it."

"If the police catch him, then maybe *I* could talk to him," his mother said. "I should have done it before, but I couldn't bring myself to ..." Her voice trailed off and they were quiet for some time.

Finally, she sighed. "Most of the time I think we just have to let it go. That's what we both need to do." She put an arm around Alex's shoulder. "But if we could know for sure ... one way or the other," she added quietly, almost to herself. "If there was only something I could do. I blame myself for not finding out the truth."

Both of them fell silent again, and then they went inside to bed. Alex's mind was still in turmoil. It had never occurred to him that his mother might blame herself. None of this was her fault.

After last night's restless sleep on the hard floor of the shed, he should have been out like a light. Instead, his mind kept replaying everything that had happened. He heard his mother breathing deeply – she was fast asleep. She'd probably spent the previous night awake, worrying about him.

Alex went over each thought, each memory, again and again. He reexperienced each emotion – the fear he'd felt when a strange man grabbed him in the old cabin; the anger when he realized who the man was; the despair when Uncle Carl left them locked on the island; the feeling of pride when he managed to swim to the other island and find the canoe; and now – the strange feeling of sorrow, the feeling that nothing was quite finished.

If Uncle Carl had found the money and escaped with it, then they'd never hear from him again. They would never know the truth of the matter. His mother would always blame herself and Alex would always wonder if he could have done more to make Uncle Carl talk to him.

But what if Uncle Carl was still on Loon Island? Maybe tomorrow the police would capture him red-handed with the money. Corporal Raynard had said he would call in a tracking dog, since the island wasn't very large.

The police would probably start by examining the holes on the east side and then the buildings at the south end where the boys had found the sleeping bag.

Alex sat up abruptly in bed. The sleeping bag! It hadn't been in Uncle Carl's boat. The tools and groceries were there, but the metal ammunition box and the sleeping bag were both gone. That meant Uncle Carl was sleeping somewhere on the island and had taken only what he could carry.

Alex lay back, his mind churning. If he were in

Uncle Carl's boots, what would he do next?

Alex threw back the covers and tiptoed across to where he'd dumped his clothes. If Uncle Carl knew the police were after him, he'd realize that tonight was his last chance to escape. There was only one way off Loon Island: the boats at Family Camp.

Alex pulled on his clothes and Jerry's boots – they'd forgotten to exchange shoes. Then he grabbed a blanket from his bed and stuffed it under his arm. He might need it. He opened the cabin door cautiously and slipped out into the dark.

A shadowy figure, sitting on the bottom step of the cabin, rose silently. Alex barely held back a shout. The shadow was Jerry.

"What're you doing here?" Alex hissed.

"Trying to figure out how to wake you up without waking anyone else," Jerry whispered. "I think your uncle is going to use a camp boat to escape. I thought I should tell you. That's what friends are for, right?"

"Right," Alex said. He knew this was Jerry's way of telling him he was forgiven. "I just figured out about my uncle too. Let's check on it."

"Should we tell the corporal what we're doing?"

"No. Not yet." Alex knew they would need the police officer eventually, but he wanted to have a few minutes alone with his uncle first. With a police officer around, his uncle might not be as willing to tell the truth. "We'll call him if we need him. Besides, he'd just send us back to bed."

Jerry had brought a flashlight, but by now the fog was completely gone and an almost full moon gave enough light for the boys to make their way over the trail and down the steps to the boathouse. They only needed the flashlight for the spots where the trees formed a canopy, blocking the moonlight.

"Let's hide here," Alex suggested, pointing to the shadow of a large boulder at the end of the steps, next to the boathouse pier. "Let's plan what to do if he shows up."

"We should have some warning," Jerry said. "We'll see his flashlight, if he uses it. And if he doesn't, we'll hear him. Your uncle doesn't know his way around the camp, does he? And you can't move quietly in the dark through all this bush."

"As soon as you hear him, sneak off and get Corporal Raynard, OK?" said Alex. He hoped that would give him enough time to get the answers he needed. "It'll take Uncle Carl a while to pick out a boat and get it ready. I'll watch him until you get back here. Then we'll capture him."

"OK," agreed Jerry, but he sounded doubtful. "I hope this works."

"It'll work," said Alex firmly. "It has to."

CHAPTER 15

ALEX SHIVERED AND pulled the blanket closer around him. Jerry dozed beside him, partly covered by the blanket. Alex turned his watch toward the moonlight that filtered through the leaves – it was almost three. Maybe they'd been wrong. Maybe this stakeout by the boathouse was a wild goose chase. Uncle Carl could have a second boat stashed somewhere. He could be miles away by now, chuckling over his escape.

A rustling sound startled Alex. Then he realized the sound was too quiet for a person to have made it. In a strip of moonlight he saw a rabbit hop out onto the edge of the pier, hesitate, and then dive back into the shadows. Once more Alex relaxed into the blanket's warmth.

A chain rattled in one of the boats and Alex jerked awake. He had dozed off. Beside him, Jerry slept too. A fine pair of detectives they made – asleep at the switch!

A muffled thump and a faint rattle sounded from the boathouse. Alex could see nothing. The moon had set behind the trees, but a faint light was beginning to brighten the east. It would be dawn soon. Alex cupped his hand over Jerry's mouth and shook him awake.

"Run for help," he whispered, his mouth beside Jerry's ear. "And no light till you're over the hill. Someone's at the boats." He saw Jerry glide away, a darker shadow among the other shadows.

Footsteps sounded in the boathouse. There was another rattle, another thump, and the scrape of a can on the floor. Alex figured he had about five minutes, maybe more, before Jerry came back with help.

Metal scraped on wood once more, followed by a distinct gurgle. Was Uncle Carl pouring fuel? The breeze carried over the smell of gasoline.

Uncle Carl must be preparing to leave. Alex remembered too late that the keys for the boats were either left in the boats or inside the boathouse, for the campers' convenience. If only he'd thought of hiding them.

Another thump sounded, as if a can had been placed on the floor. Then Alex heard another chain rattle.

He had no time to lose. He had to do something or Uncle Carl would escape. And if he escaped, Alex would never see him again and would never be able to find out what happened three years ago.

Alex slipped out of the shelter of the rock and

across the remaining few feet to the pier. He could see a fishnet piled at the corner of the boathouse. It was a large net, the kind used to pull in giant muskies and pike.

He grabbed the net and peered around the boathouse. A dark figure hunched over the rear of a boat. The figure straightened and jerked, and the motor coughed briefly. The figure paused and then climbed back out onto the boathouse pier, muttering to itself.

At that second, Alex sprang. He lifted the net high into the air and flung it down hard over his uncle's head. At the same time, he gave a running push. Uncle Carl fell backwards, his head and shoulders enveloped in the net. He grunted as he struck the edge of the boat. After lying still for a moment, he groaned and forced himself upright.

Alex crouched on the dock, struggling to hold the net down over Uncle Carl, while his uncle, swearing, pushed against it. With a sudden heave, he overpowered Alex and flung back the net. Alex half fell, still clasping the handle, and was half pulled into the center of the boat. He landed hard on the ammunition box. At once his uncle clamped the net over Alex.

"Kid, you're as much trouble as your father was!" he panted. With a sudden flash, Uncle Carl's knife slashed through the rope that held the boat to the pier. The boat floated free. He moved to the motor and jerked on the cord. The motor sputtered and came to life.

Alex freed himself from the net and leaped for the ammunition box. He clutched it under his arm and plunged into the water. The box was heavy. He sank below the surface, struggling to hold on to it. But the metal slid out of his hands and disappeared into the lake.

Jerry's heavy boots were dragging him down. Kicking frantically, Alex rose to the surface, just as Uncle Carl swung the boat back toward him and cut the motor.

"Alex! Where are you?" he shouted, leaning over the edge of the boat.

His uncle's cries startled Alex. He sank a second time, then kicked back to the surface again.

Suddenly, he realized he was not alone in the water. Uncle Carl was beside him, breathing heavily, trying to hold him up. "This way, Alex," he gasped, grabbing his arm. "Here's the boat." In the faint light it was hard to see, but the panic in his uncle's voice was plain.

"I can *swim*!" Alex protested, pushing him aside. "Let me go!" He struck out strongly for shore, and where the water became shallow, pulled himself out onto the pier.

Alex lay still, struggling to catch his breath. The next moment he felt his uncle flop down beside him.

A sudden shout came from the top of the hill. Two flashlights darted small beams here and there while running feet sounded loudly on the steps.

Alex raised his head and looked at his uncle. In the pre-dawn light, he could see the worry lines wrinkling his forehead, and the dark eyes so much like his father's.

The footsteps came closer. Uncle Carl hesitated, half rose to his knees, then slumped back down beside Alex. He sighed deeply and shook his head.

"Kid, I'm getting too old for this," he muttered. "Without the money, forget it. It's not worth it. *None* of it's worth what it's cost me already."

CHAPTER 16

CORPORAL RAYNARD, WITH Jerry hard on his heels, reached the pair on the wharf almost at once. Without a word, Uncle Carl held out his hands for the cuffs. Then, in the slowly increasing light of dawn, the four of them climbed the steps to the main lodge. The corporal called for Mrs. Barkley.

In a few minutes she bustled out, her purple housecoat ballooning around her. She stared in amazement at the group. Uncle Carl and Alex dripped puddles on the lodge floor. "I'll get some towels," she murmured and bustled off again. In a moment she returned, draped thick beach towels around them both, and hurried to the kitchen. "I'll make some hot chocolate," she said. She didn't ask any questions.

"I'll use the radio to call it in," Corporal Raynard said. He retreated briefly to Mrs. Barkley's office, taking Uncle Carl with him. The boys stood together, saying nothing. Alex couldn't bring himself to talk and even Jerry was quiet. The men returned just as Mrs. Barkley carried in a tray of steaming mugs. They sipped their hot chocolate in silence, each lost in his own thoughts.

In half an hour or so the roar of a motorboat broke the silence. A few minutes later, two more policemen strode into the lodge. "We'll question him in there," one of them said, leading Uncle Carl into the office and leaving Corporal Raynard to take statements from the boys.

About then, Mr. Wylie appeared. He stood with his hand on Jerry's shoulder while the corporal questioned the boys.

"You two shouldn't have tried that stakeout alone," Corporal Raynard said sternly. "Why didn't you wake me up?"

"We figured you wouldn't let us help," Alex said sheepishly.

The corporal asked them a string of questions and the two boys explained how they'd hidden by the boathouse but had fallen asleep. Alex described his attempt to prevent the boat from being stolen and how he'd fallen into the water during the struggle.

"It's weird, though," he said. "My uncle had the chance to get away, but he came back to save me. He thought I couldn't swim."

Finally, Alex told the officer the one thing that still mattered – that the metal box was in the lake near the boathouse dock. He felt sure it must contain the stolen money and that this might help prove his father's innocence – or part of it, anyway. If the money was there, then Uncle Carl had lied when he said he didn't know where Alex's dad had hidden the money. And if he'd lied about that, maybe he'd lied about other things too.

"We'll bring in a diver to find the box," Corporal Raynard said as the other two policemen brought Uncle Carl back to the main room of the lodge.

"He won't talk without a lawyer," one of them said. "So let's get him back to town."

Alex watched as they started to lead Uncle Carl away. He saw the slump of his shoulders, the lines of fatigue and worry on his face. His own anger, Alex realized, was mostly gone, and he felt only sorrow. Nothing could bring back his dad.

"Please," he asked Corporal Raynard, "can I talk to my uncle before you go? Alone?" The corporal nodded and all three policemen moved to the far side of the room. Jerry and Mr. Wylie went there too.

Alex struggled with the wet zipper on his jacket and reached deep into the pocket. His hands first encountered the screwdriver he'd taken from his uncle's supplies. He found what he wanted below it.

"This is yours, Uncle Carl."

A strange look passed over his uncle's face when he saw the medallion. "Where'd you get that?"

"In the clearing on the east side of Loon Island. Where you'd been digging."

"So you knew all along I'd been there?"

Alex nodded. "I wondered ..." He held out the medallion. Realizing that his uncle's hands were still cuffed, he slipped it into his uncle's pocket. "You'd better keep it. I know it was important to you."

"Thanks, kid," he said. Alex turned to walk away, but stopped when his uncle spoke again. "Wait." Uncle Carl looked down at his feet. "I gotta tell you something."

A long pause passed before Uncle Carl started speaking again. "All that stuff I said at court. That's not the way it was. Your dad didn't help me rob the bank. It was all my idea, my greed. I thought you'd figure that out, but ..."

Alex took a deep breath. "You mean my dad helped you get away and that's all?"

The lines on his uncle's face seemed to deepen. "I mean your dad was innocent of everything. He had nothing to do with *any* of it."

"But he was with you at the south end, when they caught you."

"If we'd done it together, do you think we'd have taken two boats? Your dad trailed me in his boat, trying to stop me. Trying to get me to go back and turn myself in. He caught up when I ran out of gas. That's what we were arguing about when the cops came."

Alex felt dizzy. "How could you do that to your own brother?" he asked, his voice bitter.

"You got to believe me, kid. I didn't want him to get hurt. It was an accident."

"And what about us?"

"I didn't want any of that, either. But don't think it's been easy for me, sitting in that cell knowing I was to blame."

Uncle Carl looked at him for another long moment, then nodded to the policemen. "Thanks, kid," he called back as they hustled him out the door.

Alex went back to sit beside Jerry again. His mind reeled. He'd wondered if his dad might be innocent ... hoped he could be, in some strange turn of events. But to finally hear it said aloud was different.

"I'll take you to your cabin," Mr. Wylie said. "To your mother."

Mrs. Franklin roused when she heard Alex tiptoe to his bed. She gasped when she saw his soaked hair and clothes. It took a while for him to convince her he was fine. He told her about everything that had happened and what Uncle Carl had said, whispering all the while, because

Lindsey and Beth were still asleep.

She reached out to hug him. "I should never have even considered that your dad could be guilty. For three years, I thought ..."

Alex nodded. "I know. But it wasn't your fault ... and now we know he didn't leave us. Not willingly."

Alex yawned. "There's one thing that still bothers me," he said as he settled under the covers. "Uncle Carl told *me*, but nobody else heard him. Everyone else will still think Dad was part of it all."

"Maybe," his mother said. "But we know now. And that's what matters most."

The sun was peeking through the leaves when Alex finally settled down. For the first time in days, he slept deeply.

* * *

Bright sunlight and the sound of laughter roused Alex. His watch showed two o'clock. Somewhere outside, not too far away, he could hear Lindsey and Beth giggling and his mother's quiet voice, though he couldn't hear what she said.

For some minutes he lay quietly in the bunk. It was over. The worry of the last few days, the shame and anger of the last three years, were all gone. Only a feeling of sorrow remained – sorrow for his father, sorrow even for Uncle Carl.

A growing sense of hunger forced Alex out of bed. He dressed quickly and slipped out the cabin door. His mother was sitting on a lawn chair reading, with the girls playing a little farther away. He watched them from the door. His mother looked more relaxed than he'd seen her for a long time and the girls' carefree shouts reassured him that all was well.

His mother saw him coming and reached out to him. "It's all over," she said. "The diver was here and found the box."

"With the money?"

"It's all there. And Uncle Carl got a lawyer and told the police everything."

"Everything?" Alex asked. "*Everything* ...?"

She nodded. "He really did. Your father's name is cleared. That's the main thing." She paused a moment as if she couldn't quite believe what she was saying. "I talked to the corporal. He says the bank still had a reward out for return of the money, and since you're the one who found it, it's yours ... and he says the insurance company will probably see things differently now too."

Alex nodded and then sighed deeply. It was all over. Really over. The money was recovered. His father's name was cleared. In one week his entire life had changed.

In a spruce tree nearby, a squirrel suddenly chattered loudly and a blue jay shrieked in the distance. The sun's rays felt hot after the fog of the two previous days. Abruptly, Alex came back to the present. This was Loon Island and it was their last day here. Tomorrow he would return to Kenora – but not to the way things had been. He had changed. He had a friend – a real friend – and that meant he could make other friends too. Friends who, like Jerry, would stick by him, no matter what.

The ache in Alex's stomach reminded him that it was already afternoon. "Do you think the cook could rustle me up something to eat?" he asked his mother.

She laughed. "I'm sure she will. Jerry was here about fifteen minutes ago, looking for you, and he was munching on a big hamburger."

"Great," said Alex. "I'll try for a hamburger too. And then I'll go find Jerry."

THE END

ABOUT THE AUTHOR:

Donna Firby Gamache is a retired teacher from MacGregor, Manitoba, who infuses her writing with a love of the outdoors. She has won several awards for her short stories, and her novels for young readers include *Sarah: A New Beginning* and *Spruce Woods Adventure*.

More Great Teen Fiction

978-1-897073-79-7

Fakie
by Tony Varrato

For Alex Miller, fitting in has become a matter of life and death. The unfortunate witness to a crime, Alex can't forget the things he has seen, and neither can the man he helped put in jail. His latest identity as a skateboarder in Virginia Beach is no easy ride – nosegrabs, ollies, and kickflips are all new to him. Alex has to catch on quickly to blend in – but the biggest trick he'll have to master is staying alive.

"... urgent pacing and suspenseful plot ... readers will happily power through to the wild-action finish." – *Booklist*

"Varrato draws the reader in with expert storytelling."
– *CM: Canadian Review of Materials*

"An excellent novel for male teen readers ..."
– *Library Media Connection*

**Shortlisted, Garden State Teen Book Award
– New Jersey Teen Readers' Choice**

**Shortlisted, The Golden Sower
– Nebraska's Children's Choice Literary Award**

Selected, YALSA Quick Picks

www.lobsterpress.com

More Great Teen Fiction

CD-Ring
by William T. Hathaway

Gabriel Estrada is waiting for his big break. He lives for his girlfriend and his band, Rip Chord – they keep him going when money issues get him down. But when a club owner dashes his hopes of making it big and the band's gear gets repossessed, Gabriel is lured into a counterfeiting scam by the promise of fast cash. He becomes the pawn of a ruthless criminal organization, whose corrupt operation goes beyond trafficking ripped CDs and DVDs. Can he make things right before everything he cares about goes up in flames?

www.lobsterpress.com

More Great Teen Fiction

978-1-897073-51-3

Dear Jo
The story of losing Leah ... and searching for hope
by Christina Kilbourne

Maxine and Leah used to have so much fun chatting with boys online. So what if they lied about their ages and where they lived ... it was just a web site ... just for fun. But when Leah disappeared, Max realized that they weren't the only ones telling lies online. Now Max must help the police catch an internet predator. Through her daily journal entries, she shares the horrible feeling of betrayal, the crushing loss of Leah, and the struggle to move on.

"... an all too real account of the dangers that lurk inside Internet chat rooms ..." – *The Globe and Mail*

"... powerful without being preachy." – *Children's Literature*

Winner, Manitoba Young Readers' Choice Awards

Winner, Snow Willow Award – Saskatchewan Young Readers' Choice

Shortlisted, New York State Reading Association Charlotte Award

Shortlisted, Red Cedar Award – BC Young Readers' Choice

Starred Selected, Canadian Children's Book Centre's "Best Books for Kids & Teens"

www.lobsterpress.com